# COLLATERAL
# DAMAGE

# COLLATERAL DAMAGE

## by Susan Cory

Collateral Damage © 2020

Print Edition

Published by Susan Cory



ISBN-13: 978-0-9853702-9-9

# Chapter 1

Luc's sister dropped off the box on November 19th, the day the long string of dominos would start to topple. Within a month, they'd all be lying flat.

Iris Reid and Luc Cormier were sitting on the living room sofa in their new apartment, surrounded by neatly labelled boxes. They had purchased a large Victorian house in Cambridge the previous Spring to serve as Luc's new restaurant on the first floor and their living quarters above. Iris had designed the upstairs as an open-plan loft in front and, in back, their bedroom and her one-woman architecture office.

Half a dozen mystery items were stacked on the surfboard-shaped coffee table in front of her. She unfurled the bubble wrap around what appeared to be a small guillotine and set it down with a thud. "Is this a torture device? Do we need to talk?"

Luc glanced up from his own unpacking. "Mandoline. For slicing potatoes thin." He nodded at the rest of Iris' pile. "Food mill, garlic roaster, herb razor, egg spatula and corn stripper."

"Did I ever mention that I'm a minimalist?"

Luc gave her a quick smile. "Too late."

"Lucky I designed so much extra storage in the restaurant kitchen." Iris leaned down to rub her dog Sheba's belly. As usual, the affection-junkie Basset Hound was sprawled inelegantly at her feet, paws in the air and huge ears splayed across the floor.

Luc rolled his shoulders. "We've been at this unpacking for hours. Maybe we should take a break." He waggled his eyebrows meaningfully and leaned over to give Iris a lingering kiss.

She slipped her hand around his back, returned the kiss warmly and murmured, "I don't think we've christened this room yet."

"No? We did the kitchen and the dining room. The living room must be feeling left out."

Iris thumbed the buttons on his fly just before the intercom let out a loud, disruptive chime. They exchanged blank looks as Luc shifted his hips and refastened his jeans.

When Iris checked the intercom video screen she saw a pixelated image of Luc's older sister, Mary, barely visible behind a large cardboard box.

"Sorry, I should have called first. I have some of Luc's things."

Iris buzzed her in, and Luc jogged past her and down the stairs. He climbed back up a few seconds later holding the box. Mary, looking as always like a smaller, feminine version of Luc, trailed behind.

"Mom figured that you'd now have space to store all the stuff that was in your old room."

"Why? What's she going to do with my room? It's not like she ever has guests."

"Beats me. I'm just the messenger." Mary looked around the loft. "Wow—cool space." She looked at Iris anxiously. "But you're still unpacking. Are you sure you still want all of us over for Thanksgiving next week?"

"Absolutely." Iris tried to sound enthusiastic. She needed to revise Ma Cormier's impression of her as the heathen, divorced hussy living in sin with her darling son. The fact that Luc was also divorced didn't seem to enter into the picture. "I've invited my friend Ellie's family as well, and my goddaughter's boyfriend, so the more the merrier."

Mary's eyes lit up when she noticed the latest copy of *Boston Magazine* lying out on an armchair. "Hey, the issue's out!" She read the headline out loud. *Is Luc Cormier the Best New Chef in New England?* and hooted. "You hot shot!"

Luc groaned and hid his face behind his hands.

Iris came over to reinspect the cover image: Luc's familiar features—heavy-lidded eyes, the enviable wave of blond, collar-length hair, his shy smile. "Doesn't he look smoldering in this photo?"

Mary tipped her head. "Not exactly how I think of him."

"I was trying not to look pissed off that they'd decided to show *me* instead of the plate of charred octopus I'd made specially for the cover."

"Riiiiight." Iris drawled. "Which is gonna sell more magazines—the hunky chef who's taking Boston by storm or a hunk of creatively garnished seafood? No disrespect to the late cephalopod."

While Mary flipped to the article and started reading, Luc untaped the box she'd brought and rummaged through it. He pulled out an envelope of photographs and peeked in.

Iris and Mary watched him discretely.

As Luc sifted through the pictures, an odd expression came over his face and the envelope slipped from his hands. He quickly stuffed the photos back into it and closed the box. "I think I'll go put this away."

The women exchanged curious looks.

# Chapter 2

By the following afternoon, when Luc went downstairs to start prepping for the dinner crowd, Iris could restrain herself no longer. As soon as the door at the bottom of the stairs banged shut, she sprinted back to their bedroom. The door to Luc's closet was closed, but it took no time for Iris to open it and locate the cardboard box Mary had delivered the night before. She dragged it down from the top shelf.

Curiosity was normal—right? She wanted to see his cute baby pictures, his sports trophies, his letters home from camp, but especially any interesting souvenirs from his dating past. Luc had told her a few things about Giovanna, the woman he'd married and divorced during his seven years living in Rome, but, for an attractive guy like him, there must have been other women before that. Maybe a fellow culinary school student?

Iris sat cross-legged on the hardwood floor and folded back the stiff cardboard flaps. The words: *Pandora's box—beware* fluttered through her head, but she batted them away. On top of an Ultimate Frisbee jersey and what looked like a batch of high school essays, she found the envelope that Luc had taken out the night before. It contained the old pre-digital kind of photos, a stack of sticky prints, with strips of impenetrable negatives in the back pocket. Luc had written on the front: High School-junior year. She slid out 24 shiny, borderless snapshots and slowly flipped through them.

The same gorgeous young Black woman was in every one. She looked like Zoë Kravitz. Luc was in a few shots with her, the two of them side-by-side, sharing the same tender expression. He wore long sideburns, and his girlfriend's short hair framed her delicate features. In one photo he had his arm around her shoulder and she had both arms wrapped around his waist, as if they were fused together. They looked like kids, but kids who already understood what love and passion were all about.

In another photo, the girlfriend was lying on a sofa, a massive Chemistry book propped up in front of her, and she was clearly laughing, gesturing to the photographer not to take the shot. Yet another photo showed Luc in a tie and jacket with his arm around her while she wore a graduation gown and mortarboard. Why was she graduating and he wasn't? If this was his junior year, was she a year ahead of him?

Why hadn't Luc ever mentioned her?

Why had they broken up?

Iris put the photos on the floor and dug down through another layer of the box. She found a dozen or so letters in their envelopes, held together with a brittle rubber band. They were addressed in an early, more tentative version of Luc's handwriting to an Angelique Jackson at a dorm at the University of California at Berkeley. The return address was Luc's mother's house in Cambridge. Iris leafed through the envelopes. They had all been returned, unopened, stamped "addressee unknown." She slid one envelope out of the pack and held it up to the bright light streaming in through a window. She couldn't make out anything legible through the heavy paper.

She carefully slid the letter back into the pack and placed it next to the photographs before exploring the bottom of the box. Wedged next to several Ultimate Frisbee trophies, Iris noticed a dog-eared book, *The Heart of a Woman* by Maya Angelou. In the flyleaf was the inscription: *Read this if you want to understand me better, lover. Your Angel.*

Iris felt sick. Luc had never written *her* a letter. *They* had never exchanged books.

She couldn't help wondering what had happened to Angelique. Had she gone off to college and left Luc ghosted and adrift in her wake?

# Chapter 3

I ris plunged a meat thermometer into the thigh. This turkey did not resemble the one in that famous Norman Rockwell painting. Eleven people were due to arrive in less than an hour, and the bird was still the color of Iris' skin at the end of a long New England winter. Its internal temperature had just reached a hundred and fifteen, fifty degrees short of edible. Regardless, Sheba lay positioned strategically by the oven door ready to hoover up any errant droppings.

Luc's footsteps on the staircase were a welcome sound. He strode into the kitchen in grass-stained sweats and leaned down to give Iris a kiss. "The Inman Square Death Squad triumphed again."

Sunday afternoon Ultimate Frisbee games with Luc's old high-school buddies were the only regular exercise he could fit in these days, what with the new restaurant needing his full attention.

"Way to go, Champ. Did you score a lot of points?" Iris had been to a few of their games but found it about as interesting to watch as grass growing—as she found most spectator sports.

"We slaughtered them." Luc sniffed the air. "What time did you say everyone was coming?"

"In an hour. I need serious triage with this bird. It's not cooking fast enough."

Luc slid the pan out of the oven, jiggled one of the legs, then put it back in. He turned up the heat. "I'm heading back for a quick shower. Why don't you get changed? I'll help you with the potatoes and gravy."

On her way to the bedroom, Iris stopped to survey the setting she'd laid out earlier on the heavy pine table, using its two extra leaves to extend it full-length. She'd had to search frantically through the last of the unopened moving boxes to locate her Murano glass candlesticks. Together with them, the oval pottery plates set against the red tablecloth made for a dramatic effect. Her friend, Ellie, would soon bring one of her creative flower centerpieces along with some vegan-friendly dishes for Iris' goddaughter, Raven, and her new boyfriend.

During the recent renovation of the apartment, Iris had removed the walls between the living and dining rooms, and the five tall windows wrapping around three sides of the room made the combined space feel open and airy. The room's proportions had been tweaked into architectural perfection. She'd added a gas fireplace to one end of the living room side and had it turned on tonight, crackling silently and invitingly.

"I've never seen matte white appliances with bronze hardware before." Raven enthused as she examined the kitchen. "Aren't these fabulous, Ash?"

Ashley Burke, the new boyfriend, was running his hand along the heavy refrigerator handle.

"Very sculptural."

As Iris crushed the boiled potatoes with a masher, she shot a sidelong glance at the striking-looking young man with light brown shoulder-length dreadlocks and piercing blue eyes. "Are you a painter too?"

"I've done sculpture, installations, other stuff, but yeah, I'm mostly painting these days." He looked at Raven. "Might be this good woman's influence."

Raven returned the look, and Iris quickly averted her eyes from its obvious intensity. They were an attractive couple. Raven was tall and willowy, with her short hair gelled out in tufts. They both wore multiple shirts, multiple earrings, tight jeans, and long scarves around their necks, as if there were a dress code for artists.

When Luc entered the kitchen, Raven hugged him and said, "Is *this* (with a sweeping gesture and a bow toward him) the best new chef in New England?"

Luc rolled his eyes. "Do you know how much grief I've been getting from my friends? They've been filling the restaurant Facebook page with memes and gifs."

Raven playfully punched him on the shoulder and introduced him to Ash. The two men exchanged a laid-back bro' handshake. Luc checked on the turkey. Considering it done, he pulled it out of the oven and set it on the counter.

"Can I help with anything?" Ash asked. "My assignment at home was always to play sculptor and carve the bird."

Luc handed him the carving fork and knife. "Sure. Let's let it rest for half an hour, then you can have at it."

Raven stage-whispered to Ash, "You know, the hot-shot chef here usually does that."

Luc raised his palms. "I'm off duty tonight."

Ellie wandered in, holding a ceramic bowl covered with plastic wrap. "Does your quinoa salad need to be refrigerated, Raven?"

A few minutes later, Luc herded everyone into the living room and proceeded to fill everyone's wine glasses with a garnet-colored Pinot Noir.

The doorbell rang and Luc went down to help his mother walk slowly up the stairs. Luc's father, a policeman, had been killed twenty years ago, and the loss had prematurely derailed his mother. Only in her late sixties, she looked a decade older. Her health had suffered from years of inactivity and little motivation. Helping his sister take care of her was a big factor in Luc's return to Cambridge after his years of living in Rome.

Luc took his mother's coat and a parcel she'd been holding and led her toward one of Iris' leather Le Corbusier chairs. As she sunk into it she said, "That's the sweet potatoes with marshmallows. You'll need to heat that up and finish it under the broiler." Luc smiled at the familiar instructions.

Mary soon clattered up the stairs with her two teenaged daughters, Louisa and Anna, in tow. All three of them had the light blond Cormier hair, but Iris could tell the girls apart because Louisa now had a conspicuous set of braces. The girls each carried a pie.

Mary set a paper bag down on the front hall table. "Tom's parking out back. He'll be up in a minute. I brought the can of cranberry sauce. Iris, nobody remembers when this stupid tradition started, but we always have to provide this weird jellied cylinder to lie in a fancy bowl at Thanksgiving. Mom's the only one who ever eats any of it. My girls won't go near it."

Mrs. Cormier called out from her seat, "I heard that! It's the *most important* thing to serve with turkey. And you have to be able to see the ridges from the can."

Luc patted his sister's shoulder. "Don't worry, Sis. I made that orange-cranberry relish you like." He introduced Ellie's group to his family and collected a large inventory of heavy coats.

Before long everyone was deep into any number of conversations. Louisa and Anna chatted about school with their grandmother while their eyes kept traveling toward Ashley. Mary's husband, Tom, debated gardening strategies and local politics with Ellie's husband, Mack. Ellie tried subtly to draw out Ash's life story. Iris gave Raven a curated tour of the apartment, describing what she had renovated, which was mostly everything.

"Who's reading Mary Oliver?" Ash picked up the book off

the coffee table and started to leaf through it. "I love her poems."

Luc smiled. "Iris just gave that to me. I can't wait to have time to read it."

Ten minutes later, when Ash carried to the table a platter with an elegant fan of evenly sliced turkey, everyone praised his carving skills. Luc said, "You can have a job plating in my restaurant anytime." Wine flowed freely and the high-ceilinged room filled with happy noise.

After everyone had filled their plates, Iris turned to Ash. "Raven told me you grew up in Medford. How did you like it?"

"Do you know the city?"

"Just the area around Tufts."

"I grew up in West Medford, along the Mystic River in an area called The Ville. It was a great place to be a kid. My father ran a boxing club there where a lot of young kids spent their time in the ring instead of getting pulled into gangs."

Iris couldn't help noticing that Ash's powerful build suggested a lot of time working out himself. "Are you living at home now?"

"No, I'm camping out in a warehouse space on Harvard Avenue, near the house my mom still owns. It's my painting studio, but I've set up a bed there. I put in a bathroom and some appliances to make up a kitchen, but it's hard to find time to work on finishing it up with all my school deadlines."

Raven joined the conversation, which she'd been listening in on. "It's unheated."

"Yeah, I'll have to do something about that before it gets much colder. I wouldn't want my paints to freeze."

"Or your girlfriend."

Luc's mother glared at Raven, who returned the look, half a smile twitching her mouth.

"Shouldn't your landlord be providing heat?" Iris asked.

"That's the problem. *I'm* the landlord. When my father died last year, I got a bit of money from his life insurance and was able to buy the building cheap. But I've run out of cash to fix it up. I'd like to subdivide it into several artists' studios."

Iris set her wineglass down. "I'm sorry to hear that your Dad passed away."

"Yeah. He was a good guy."

"If you need an architect's ideas on ways to get heat into your building, I'd be glad to take a look at it."

"Really? That would be awesome."

It seemed like such an inconsequential offer, which only went to show how wrong Iris could be.

# Chapter 4

Six days later, a purply dusk was settling in to the west as Iris pulled up in front of Ash's brick warehouse across from an automotive repair shop. The one-story structure took up fifty feet of frontage on Medford's busy Harvard Avenue. Ash was talking on his cell phone, his breath visible in puffs as he waited for her on the sidewalk. He turned and approached the Jeep, and Iris lowered the window.

"Am I OK parking here?"

"Sure. It's the Wild West out here. You're not in Cambridge anymore."

After an awkward handshake, Iris followed Ash past a row of metal windows that probably did little to keep out the cold. In a jingle of keys, he unlocked the steel street door.

Ash flipped a switch and industrial lights lit up a big open space punctuated lengthwise by tall wood posts every dozen feet. Large wooden trusses supported an exposed plank ceiling.

Iris looked around. "What a fantastic building. Looks like around three thousand square feet? What was it used for?"

"Making bricks. Medford was famous for them in the eighteenth and nineteenth centuries. This is just part of the original factory. You can see the outlines of some of the old kilns out back. The drying yard was built over. They used to load the bricks on barges and float them down the Mystic River to Boston. The Tufts family owned a big brickyard where the college is now."

Ash led her over to the far wall where he'd built a partition around what was probably a bathroom, against which ran a rudimentary galley kitchen. Iris could smell the scent of fresh oil paint.

"Would you like some coffee?"

"Sure, thanks."

Ash took an espresso pot down from an open shelf while Iris continued looking around.

His few pieces of furniture consisted of a duvet-covered mattress on the floor in a corner and a lone thrift-shop easy chair. Carpentry tools, paints and brushes were neatly organized in bins on open metal shelves which also housed a collection of books. An old wooden desk sat beneath one of the tall windows next to eight large canvases stacked up on a metal shelf against the wall and covered with a clear plastic tarp. A framed picture on the desk showed a teenaged Ash with an older man, both kitted out in boxing gear. The boy was grinning, his eyes sparkling with excitement.

"Is this your father?" Iris called over.

Ash looked over his shoulder to what Iris was holding. "Uh,

huh. That's my old man, Tavis Burke."

Iris put the photo back. She wandered over to an unfinished painting set up on an easel. Against a saturated blue background, she could make out an abstract collage of several men's profiles ripped from newspapers and wearing folded paper hats. Painted messily next to them was the simple outline of a man's face, black on one half with blue showing through its opposite side. In the background was a forest of hieroglyphics which Iris couldn't begin to interpret.

Ash came up alongside her, holding two cups of espresso. "I hope you like it this way. No milk or sugar today, sorry."

"Thanks." Iris took the cup. "Your work is really good. I like the mixed media part."

He tilted his head and studied the piece. "This one isn't finished. It's for an assignment due on Monday to make a self-portrait. I've been experimenting with different textures and layers, mixing abstract and representational."

"I thought that head was you. I'm not sure that I can make out all the background symbols though."

"That's actually a fantasy map of the Ville showing important places from when I was little."

Iris sipped her coffee. "You have a lot of talent."

"Thanks. I'm a senior now at UMass Boston. Raven thinks I should try to get signed up with a dealer right after graduation."

"What do *you* want to do?"

"I'd rather get this place fixed up first, subdivide it into a couple of lofts to share with some other artists. Then I can move ahead and try to scratch out a career as a painter. But I guess that's ass-backwards. I'll need to make a lot of money first in order to make this place livable."

Iris looked around at all the leaky windows and uninsulated walls. The words "uphill battle" came to mind. Still, an idea niggled at the back of her mind. She stared at the high wood ceiling on its rugged trusses, the weathered brick walls. The space had a certain poetry to it. "Maybe there's a way to interest the Harvard or MIT Architecture schools in using this warehouse as a case study. They could design solar panels or a wind turbine to provide heat and power to get your building to reach Passive House or LEED Platinum standards, using ultra-low amounts of energy to operate. An urban retrofit project like this would be right up their alley. The standard, crunchy-granola Vermont solar house is old news. The schools would be able to use this as a teaching tool while you might get a free heating system put in."

Ash jerked his chin back in surprise. "Like a reality TV show? Do you really think they'd be interested?"

"Let's find out." Iris fished her phone out of her purse. "Do you mind if I take some pictures to show them?"

# Chapter 5

After Iris was finished photographing the building, Ash suggested that they get a bite to eat. She normally dined alone on Saturday nights, most nights really, one drawback of being romantically involved with a professional chef. The Healthy Planet café Ash suggested was around the corner from the studio. It was not what she'd expected. Far from having a new-age, Scandinavian-looking interior, it resembled a crowded neighborhood burger joint, without offering any actual burgers. Strands of Christmas tree lights were looped along the tops of the windows, casting a multi-colored glow. The Christmas carols playing in the background were almost drowned out by the animated conversations of the mixed crowd—old timers, young families and a sprinkling of hipsters.

Ash greeted several people as he and Iris threaded their way to a red Naugahyde booth in the back. A matronly waitress wiped down their table, dispensing menus from her apron pocket. "Hey, Ash. You having your regular?"

"Give us a minute, Maggie. Iris needs to study the choices."

Ash's own menu stayed closed. "I recommend the buffalo tofu bowl or the soy wraps. This used to be a typical old greasy spoon coffee shop, but Maggie turned it into a healthy place to eat. The regulars grumbled, but they're still here."

Iris worried *did a tuna sandwich qualify as vegan?* By the time Maggie, the owner-cum-waitress returned, Iris had settled on a bowl of mushroom soup.

"I probably eat here—" Ash stopped and a wide grin stretched across his face. Iris turned to follow his gaze.

A bald Black man, maybe in his fifties, was heading slowly toward their table. His skin was tinged with yellow and his cheeks looked hollowed out.

Ash stood up and hugged him. "Come join us. This is Iris Reid, an architect who's helping me get my studio up to speed." He gestured to the bald guy. "Bruno Thomas is a family friend."

Bruno flapped his hand. "I don't want to interrupt." He gave Iris an anemic handshake. "Nice to meet you. Maggie made me some soup for takeout. Ash, I hope you're finding time to work out. You don't want to let your boxing skills get rusty."

Ash laughed. "I wish I could squeeze it in. My professors keep me pretty busy. How are you feeling?"

"Tired." Bruno shrugged. "I'm running out of gas. Your mother in Haiti again?"

"Uh, huh. She'll be back for Christmas."

"She's truly an Angel to do that every year." Bruno turned

and walked slowly toward the counter, waggling his fingers in a goodbye wave.

Ash called after him, "Take care of yourself." His eyes followed Bruno's leisurely procession. "The doctors didn't catch his Hep C early enough for a liver transplant. Bruno's got a ton of miles on him for a guy not even forty."

*That guy wasn't much older than Luc? Hard to believe.*

Maggie returned, balancing plates along her arm. Ash's blobs of tofu, sitting on a bed of brown rice, were suspiciously orange. But after Iris took a sip of her soup, she had to concede that someone in the kitchen knew what they were doing.

"What was Bruno saying about your mother going to Haiti?" she asked.

"For the last few years she's gone there for three weeks with some other nurses and doctors from Boston Medical. They help out at a clinic in a village near Cap Haitien. My grandmother still lives nearby."

"Have you ever been?"

"Four or five times. I've done a series of portraits of some of the people I've met there. There's a glow about them. They may be dirt poor and surrounded by corruption, but the spirit of the people is amazing. And the music, the colors…" Ash closed his eyes.

"I'd love to see those paintings. Is there one of your grandmother?"

The wail of a fire truck pierced through the restaurant's plate-glass windows. Red lights raced past, then halted abruptly, still strobing. A second pump truck followed close behind.

Ash stood up to see better. "Shit, that's my studio." He reached into his pocket for his wallet.

"I've got this. Go! I'll catch up." Iris put some bills on the table and slipped her arms into her parka.

As soon as she was out the door, she could smell it. What looked like low clouds hovered above the warehouse. She caught up to Ash in front of the building and they watched, horrified, as the clouds burst into angry yellow flames that lit up the dark sky.

"No!" Ash shouted as he ran toward the front door.

A fire fighter blocked his path.

"This is my property. What happened? How?"

"Anyone inside? Any chemicals or flammables?" the man shouted.

"No, it's empty. We were at dinner, but it was fine an hour ago. My paintings and some oil paint are in there. Some turpentine too. Oh, and a roll of canvas." Ash moved toward the door again.

"You can't go in." The fireman pulled Ash by the arm over to talk with a man who was issuing orders.

Iris watched the flames, fascinated and sick. A man with a hose was being hoisted up on a ladder from the first truck. Responders were unspooling the rest of the hose from the second truck. The fire seemed to be concentrated in the roof above Ash's living quarters. She could imagine the wood trusses, columns, and plank ceiling acting as kindling to fuel the flames. The fireman on the ladder shot arcs of water through the air. Iris thought guiltily about how beautiful it looked.

The Fire Chief was relaying information from Ash directly into his shoulder microphone. "No civilians inside… building's mainly empty… tubes of oil paint and a tin of turpentine in corner of origin." The chief looked at Ash. "You got a working sprinkler system in there?"

Ash nodded. "Yeah."

There was squawking coming through the phone. The chief said, "You sure?" then gave Ash a steady look. "It didn't activate."

"But… I bought the property a few months ago, and it passed inspection."

"Well, it didn't work tonight. You got the keys to the front and back doors? We've got to open up the place, get the fans going."

In a daze, Ash pulled two keys off a large ring and handed them to the chief.

Iris startled at a whooshing sound as a section of charred roof came crashing down to the floor, setting off a cascade of sparks through the gaping new opening. She felt a burst of intense heat and stepped backward. Ash stared up at the collapsed roof, his fingers steepled over his mouth.

Several firefighters, sweat pouring down their faces, rolled two huge fans off one of the trucks and wheeled them toward the front door. Iris scanned the growing crowd and recognized some of the people she'd seen in the restaurant, now wearing mesmerized expressions.

An older man with a white crewcut and weatherbeaten skin approached the Fire Chief. They talked in low voices, glancing over at Ash. A fireman hurried out of the building, over to the chief and handed him something. The two men raised the object to their noses, then exchanged looks. Crew cut sealed it in a bag. He wore a windbreaker with no identifying logo.

Crewcut strolled over to Ash. "My name is Phil Weaver. I'm the State Fire Marshall. The Deputy Chief tells me you live in this building. You squatting?"

Ash rose to his full six feet and glared at the man. "I own this property."

Iris added her own glare.

The intensity of her look had crewcut turn to her. "And who are you?"

"Iris Reid, an architect. I'm here consulting on renovations to the building." *Close enough.*

"We'll need a complete statement from you, Ms. Reid." He faced Ash again. "Do you have ID?"

Ash's face darkened. "Do you always ask building owners for ID when their building's on fire?"

"In certain circumstances I do."

"You mean the sprinklers?"

"Among other things."

# Chapter 6

On Sunday morning Iris sat in the living room of Ellie's house, two blocks from Iris' new apartment. Ash and Raven lay sprawled on the sofa. Ash, dressed in a set of Mack's too-large sweats, looked like he'd barely slept. Raven worked distractedly on her laptop.

Iris fanned out twenty 8" x 10" photos on the coffee table next to several abandoned coffee mugs and half-eaten plates of eggs and bagels. "Is there anything useful here?" She said to the group. "I was too tired last night to do anything more than forward them to you, Ellie."

It had been after eleven by the time she and Ash had watched the fire die down and answered all the Fire Marshall's probing questions. As soon as Raven had heard the news, she'd driven back from the Rhode Island School of Design to meet Ash at her parents' house, so they could get some sleep and figure out next steps.

"I guess this one is proof that *I* didn't set the fire." Ash pushed across a photo showing the sprinkler control box by the entry door. "The padlock was fine when we left for dinner. But an hour later the firemen found it smashed. Someone disabled the system so it wouldn't alert the Fire Department that the water valve had been shut off."

"The arsonist must have broken in soon after you left," Ellie said. "But who'd want to torch your building?"

"I've been awake most of the night trying to figure that out. It's not like I have enemies. There're some guys I beat in boxing matches when I was younger, but no one carried a grudge." Ash rubbed his face.

Raven put her arm around his shoulders. "We're all gonna help, babe. Look here. I pulled up the Medford Fire Department's Twitter feed."

**MEDFORD FIRE DEPT.@MEDFORDMAFIRE**

BREAKING: Firefighters respond to 20 Harvard Avenue for a 2 alarm fire. Arson suspected. No injuries.

UPDATE: A reward of up to $2000 offered to anyone who can help identify the person responsible for setting last night's fire at 20 Harvard Avenue between 6:30 and 7 P.M.

"Sounds like you're in the clear, Ash," Raven said. "You were with Iris then and lots of people saw you in the restaurant." Raven tapped more keys, then passed her laptop to Iris. "What do you think?"

Iris saw the candid photo she'd taken of Ash facing his self-portrait. A heading read "Medford artist burned out of his studio. Please help!" Raven had already set up a GoFundMe site to help keep Ash on his feet and to subsidize the rebuilding.

"But won't your insurance cover that?" Iris asked.

"If I *had* insurance, but I needed all the money from my father's insurance just to buy the building outright. No bank would've given a loan to a broke college student like me." Ash's eyes looked moist. "All of my paintings were destroyed."

"Let's call the Fire Department to find out when you can get back inside. I can help you figure out how much damage was actually done. The brick walls may still be structurally sound. It takes a lot of heat to burn masonry and those firemen got there right away. Maybe we can still interest Harvard or M.I.T. in turning it into a studio project for green architecture."

Ash raised his head. "Even after all the destruction?"

"That might give the students even more latitude for showcasing new products or design ideas. I'm not saying it will fly, but I'll sure try to spin it that way."

Ash gave Iris a grateful look. "If you hadn't been with me last night, taking these photos and vouching for me, I might be in jail right now. That Fire Marshall was jonesing to pin arson on me."

Iris remembered her own night locked in a holding cell eight months before. A con artist had set her up to look like a participant in a bank robbery where a guard had gotten shot. "Seeing you installed in your renovated studio will be my thanks. Besides, without insurance on the building you'd have no incentive to burn it down."

Raven handed Ash the photo with his self-portrait. "We'd better go down to my studio so you can try to recreate this. It's due tomorrow, right? I've gotta work on a painting myself." Raven mouthed a silent "thank you" to Iris as she passed.

Ellie handed Iris a fresh mug of coffee as an explosion of music emanated from the basement, bass notes thumping. "It's nice of you to spend so much time helping Ash."

"I thought it would only be an hour or two giving him some construction advice."

"Are you sure you want to shop his building project around to Harvard and M.I.T.? It'll take some effort to put together a presentation to them."

Iris drained her mug and set it down carefully on the coffee table. "I feel bad for the poor kid. He was trying to be practical and buy some property, only to have some despicable person try to destroy it. That kind of unfairness makes me crazy. And you should have heard how the Fire Marshall was treating him—asking him if he was a squatter."

"Oh, God." Ellie shook her head. "He mentioned that his mother's off the grid in Haiti volunteering at a clinic until Christmas. I don't get the sense that she can help financially, anyway."

"And now I've gotten his hopes up about renovating his building with donated labor and materials. I sure hope I can deliver. Do you have any contacts these days at M.I.T.? I'd rather not deal with Gilles at Harvard after the bastard fired me from the Faculty Guest House project."

"I'm sure he regrets that now. Spring term starts in late January for Harvard and February for M.I.T. so you'd be lucky if all the studios aren't already assigned. My contacts have all moved on. You'll have to plead your case directly with the Deans. But don't you have any deadlines for your own work?"

"I've been turning stuff down all fall. After all the press I got for designing Luc's restaurant, everyone wants me to clone the design for their own places. Besides, I just closed on the old Washington Avenue house so I'm feeling flush. I thought I'd take a break for a while. Finish the details on our new place."

"Are you OK about selling your house? I know you weren't sure about selling versus renting it out."

"My parents' ghosts will probably come back to haunt me, but it feels like the right decision."

"So no regrets about moving in with Luc?"

Iris hesitated. She still hadn't told Ellie what her snooping had uncovered about Luc's high school girlfriend. *Why did such ancient history bother her, anyway?* "Given the hours he's putting in, it's the only way we'd have any quality time together. Plus, he's just learned that he's in the running for a James Beard award, so that will mean he'll have even less free time."

Ellie gave her a concerned look.

"The only one not on board with the move is Sheba," Iris continued quickly. "She keeps pulling on her leash toward the Washington Avenue house. And if I take her there, she sits on the sidewalk staring back and forth from the house to me with those sad Bassett hound eyes."

"Sounds stressful all around."

"I'm using the house proceeds to pay down the mortgage on our new place. I want to be all in with Luc."

Ellie's eyes widened. "That's…uh…"

"A big commitment, I know. But I want to share everything with Luc. This time everything is going to work out."

# Chapter 7

Later that afternoon, as Ash and Iris pulled up to his warehouse, he squinted up at the roof. "Who's that guy up there?" He scrambled out of the Jeep. "Hey!" He yelled, hands on his hips.

The whine of a power screwdriver stopped abruptly and a young man with a long braid, wearing leather pants, looked up from affixing a large sheet of plywood.

Iris waved at him and called up, "So, we get the big boss, huh?"

Milo replied with a grin and a thumbs-up. "I guess I need to get more of a life on weekends. Give me a few minutes to finish this and I'll meet you inside."

Iris turned to Ash. "I figured you'd want the holes covered to protect the place from the weather and possible break-ins, so I called a contractor friend of mine who owes me a favor."

"Oh, wow, good idea. Thanks for thinking of that."

"Let's take a quick look around and I'll take more photos to document the damage, OK?"

Ash turned the key in the lock and they stepped inside. He moaned. Half the windows were broken, the brick walls were covered in soot, and the wood plank ceiling over his studio area was burned completely through. Water lay in filthy puddles on the concrete floor.

He headed for his paintings in the far corner, Iris close behind. The protective plastic tarp had melted into a bubbled mess across most of the top canvases. Ash pushed it to one side and slid out the next two paintings. The paint on them was blistered, and the canvases were blackened around the edges. "Shit!" Ash dumped them onto a discard pile and pulled out two more to lay on the floor. They seemed much heavier and were painted on a harder surface.

Iris peered over his shoulder. "Those look kind of cool."

Ash held one up to examine it closely. "Hmm. I ran out of canvas and painted on MDF instead. It's like plywood with a smooth face. I guess it wasn't as affected by the extreme heat as the other ones. And these were protected under several layers of paintings."

The paint had crackled somewhat around the edges, but the abstract patterns were still clearly visible.

Ash pulled out the last two and studied them. "I think I can salvage these four. They're different from what I'd intended, but I think I kind of like them."

"You could start a new art movement and bake all your work in a kiln from now on," Iris said.

Ash raised his eyebrows. "Like forgers do to make their

copies look like Old Masters?"

Iris cracked a sideways smile. "But seriously, you're lucky the stack was up off the floor. Otherwise, they would've been trashed by all the water the firemen sprayed in here. Let's put those four good paintings in the back of my Jeep. We can store them at Ellie's or at my place while your building's being worked on."

"I can leave them at my mother's house around the corner."

Milo came up behind them. "All buttoned up. Hey, did you paint those? So this is an art studio?"

Iris introduced Milo and Ash. The two shook hands and sized each other up. Milo, whose arm displayed an impressive snake tattoo emanating from the sleeve of his t-shirt to his wrist, played in a rock band in his off-hours. He flipped his braid over a shoulder. "Do they know how this fire started?" Milo asked Ash.

"It looks like arson," Ash said. "Someone destroyed my sprinkler system before setting the roof on fire."

"That's really messed up," Milo said. "But your insurance will cover the repair work—right?"

Ash shoved his hands in his pockets and shook his head. "I don't have any insurance."

Milo raised his eyebrows and looked at Iris.

Ash continued, "Iris is going to try to get some architecture students to help with the rebuilding, you know, as a school project."

Milo looked amused. "Is she?"

"Well, 'try' being the operative word." *Was this a ridiculous idea? Why was Milo grinning at her like that?*

Iris turned away, fished her phone out of her pocket and started walking around, photographing the scene.

Milo trailed after her while Ash went back to scrutinizing his baked paintings.

She made a circuit of the interior. "What do you think, Milo? Is the building still structurally sound?"

He tapped his hammer against some bricks on the most heavily scorched walls. "Seems solid enough." He cast a glance up at the ceiling directly over the painting studio and pointed. "You're gonna have to repair the wood truss up there. And fill in the wood plank ceiling, unless you're intending to add insulation. But it'd be a shame to cover it up. And I don't know how you're gonna repair those old steel windows that got smashed. Maybe they can be straightened out and re-welded. You can get new ones, but they cost a fortune. Most of the other damage is superficial—the soot and water stains should come off with a good power washing." He gave her a wink. "Your students should be able to patch this place up in no time."

Even though she knew he was making fun of her, she couldn't help grinning back. They had become friends while working on Luc's restaurant together. After his crew had finished work on their apartment and cleared out, she'd missed seeing him every day. "You've been a big help." She reached in her purse for her checkbook. "Thanks for coming to the rescue on a Sunday. Let me write you a check."

Milo shrugged. "No charge. This is my contribution to the art world." He walked over to Ash and shook his hand. "Good luck with everything."

"Thanks, man."

After Milo left, she and Ash stood by the front door staring at the broken padlock on the sprinkler control box.

"This wasn't random," Iris said. "Someone planned this. They knew there was an alarm attached to the sprinkler system and how to disable it. They also knew how to get in and when you'd be gone. Who have you let inside?"

It took a minute for the implications to sink in before Ash said, "It couldn't have been someone I know. I've only let in Raven and my Mom. And the seller and the broker both saw the new alarm at the closing. Maybe they told someone. Oh, and Maggie stopped by with a bottle of champagne. Or someone might have been able to see in through the windows." Ash looked confused. "But I don't understand what anyone would gain. If the firemen hadn't gotten here so quickly, the whole building could've burned down. Who would benefit then?"

"Was there anyone else interested in getting hold of this property? How did you learn about it?"

"The guy who owns the auto shop across the street used to use this building to store car parts. I grew up just around the corner and my Dad's boxing club was a block away so I always passed by this place. After I got the money from Dad's insurance, I talked Frank, the owner, into selling me the place. It wasn't officially for sale."

"Let's go talk with Frank. See if anyone else ever approached him about buying it."

"Do you think someone's trying to scare me into selling?"

Iris shrugged. "Or maybe someone hopes you run out of money and need to sell a damaged building on the cheap."

"But if anyone approached me now with an offer, wouldn't I know that they were behind the fire?"

"Maybe they'll try to wait you out."

Iris thought but didn't add *or maybe they'll make a more successful attempt.*

# Chapter 8

Iris wasn't sure how she'd ended up again at the almost-empty Healthy Planet café, sitting in the same booth as the night before. This place seemed to be Ash's home-away-from-home. He'd insisted on taking her there to thank her for all of her help.

"They have real coffee here—right?" Iris asked tentatively. "Not just green tea or chai?"

Ash laughed. "Yes, they have real coffee. Maggie's even got a pretty good espresso machine. We are somewhat civilized here in beautiful downtown Medford."

Maggie bustled over when she saw Ash. "Oh Sweetie, I'm so sorry about your building. What a terrible thing." She gave his shoulder a squeeze. "Is your Mom flying back?"

Ash's face turned somber. "I can only reach her on the hospital's SAT phone and it's not like there's anything she can do. She might as well stay in Haiti and finish her time there."

"Well, let me know if there's anything I can do to help." Maggie took out two laminated menus from her apron pocket, but Ash waved them away.

He looked questioningly at Iris. "Just coffee?"

After taking Iris' order for a Macchiato and Ash's for an oat Matcha latte, Maggie headed off to the kitchen. She was a large woman with wild brown hair that resembled a bird's nest sitting on top of her head. Her face was soft and cherubic.

"She seems to know you well," Iris said.

"Maggie's been friends with my mother for ages. Bruno and Maggie went to high school with my mom and I went to school with their son, Jamal."

"This place is like the TV show, 'Cheers'."

He looked at her blankly.

"Before your time. I didn't realize that Bruno and Maggie were a couple."

"Yeah, I guess they met as teenagers. They've had a lot of ups and downs, especially with Jamal. He got into drugs, been in and out of rehab. Bruno tried to get him to take boxing classes in my father's club when he was a kid. That worked for a while until Jamal discovered drugs. I think they've fried his brain cells." Ash raked a hand through his hair. "My Mom said that Bruno was also way deep into drugs when he was younger, but he found a way to kick them, so maybe, hopefully, Jamal will get straightened out."

Maggie returned and set down their drinks, along with a plate of cookies. "My famous molasses cookies. Your favorite. You need to keep up your strength to get through this."

Ash shot her a grateful smile and reached for the plate.

★　★　★

Iris followed Ash's directions and pulled the Jeep up in front of a small nearby cottage with a well-kept lawn, set back from the street. It was painted in artistic shades of green, tan and salmon which, surprisingly, didn't clash.

"Great house. I love the colors."

"My mother let me choose them ten years ago when it was time to repaint the place. I've always had strong opinions about color combinations."

Ash unloaded his backpack and the replacement self-portrait he'd brought from Cambridge along with the four salvaged paintings from the trunk of Iris' car. He handed her two of the paintings to carry. He fumbled the key into the lock and they entered directly into a cozy living room centered by a brick fireplace.

"This is home." Ash reached down to collect the mail that had been dropped in through the mail slot. "At least until I can get my studio set up again. We can stack the canvases here against the wall for now."

Iris set down her load and looked around. The place had a comfortable level of domesticity—a stack of magazines, paintings that looked like they might be from Haiti, a large bookcase—without being too cluttered. A semi-abstract portrait hung over the mantlepiece. It depicted a beautiful woman in loose stylized strokes. "This is one of yours, isn't it?"

"Um, yeah. One of the few that didn't burn. It's of my mother."

"It's stunning."

"Thanks. She actually doesn't like having a picture of herself front-and-center, but I think she leaves it here because I painted it when I was in high school."

"You two sound pretty close."

"We are. It was just the two of us until I was six."

Iris looked back at the painting, at the strength and beauty in the woman's face. "She must be an incredible woman."

# Chapter 9

Iris called the M.I.T. office first thing on Monday morning and was put through directly to Dean Aki Hayasaki. Iris went through her pitch but the Dean, regretfully, was not able to offer any spring studio course that still needed a project focus. "This fire-damaged artist's studio sounds like a worthy effort. I do hope you find a sponsor."

After hanging up, Iris slammed her palm down on the desk, startling Sheba awake from her customary spot at Iris' feet. *Damn.* That left calling Gilles at Harvard. Iris flushed with anger at the memory of the last time they'd spoken, when he'd fired her, pointing out that her tarnished personal reputation reflected poorly on dear old Harvard. The pompous ass! Even after she was later fully vindicated by the police and the *Boston Globe,* he'd never called back to apologize. Plus, he'd let that hack, Vernon Elliott, redesign her Harvard Square project and ruin it altogether.

Iris wandered into the kitchen to toast herself a bagel. Anger and humiliation made her hungry. Surely the Harvard professors would also have their spring courses planned by now. Why put herself through making nice with the abominable Gilles and begging him for a favor?

She headed back to her home office with her plate and sat down at her desk, staring out the window at the large Linden tree swaying in the wind. She took a bite of her bagel. Dean Hayasaki had said something that had stuck in her mind. "I do hope you find a *sponsor.*" A sponsor didn't need to be a school. What if she presented this project to a magazine? She had an "in" with the leading trade magazine, *Architecture Now!* It could be their Green showcase of the year. Companies might line up to donate their products for the exposure. She could do the design part. It would be great publicity and they might even pay her. Of course she'd need to hire a contractor to actually do the work. She wondered if Milo was busy.

Iris spent the next hour researching eco-companies: Wide-plank flooring recycled from barns—check. Bamboo cabinets for the kitchenettes—check. Energy-efficient appliances and water-saving fixtures—check. New energy-efficient triple-paned steel windows—check. Hemp insulation for the walls—check. Smart skylights with integrated LED lighting—check.

She wondered if her old classmate Barb would donate one of her company's geo-thermal heating and air conditioning systems. After all, Barb owed her. Iris was responsible for her becoming Meeker Enterprise's CEO.

But most of these products were already well known. She needed something sexier, more innovative to draw the magazine's interest. She continued to scroll through the web. Twenty minutes later she found it: Harcon Glass solar roof shingles. Eureka! And adding solar shingles would solve the need to reroof as well. There was even some miracle coating on them that created an impressive R-50 insulation value. Surely Alex Harcon, the brilliant playboy billionaire responsible for all kinds of sustainable, well-designed luxury products, would love to be associated with an artsy project like this. Especially with the human interest angle of some evil arsonist depriving a photogenic young artist of his precious, hard-won workplace. She'd have to remember to include the photo of Ash gazing thoughtfully at his own self-portrait.

Iris opened Photoshop and loaded the pre-fire photographs she'd taken of the exterior of the warehouse. She edited in a facsimile of the glass roof tiles and new, sharp-looking steel windows. She played around with the image, cropping it, adding a dark green front door, making the sky brighter. Then she added a sign by the entry: *Architecture Now! Artists' Lofts*.

Once she was satisfied with the image, she went on to write up a proposal, listing the companies that might be cajoled into donating various materials. Now she felt ready to approach her contact at the magazine, its editor, Harmony Jensen. Their rival, *cuttingedgedecor*, had featured a house that Iris had designed on its cover the previous year, and ever since then *Architecture Now!* had been lobbying for its own chance to publish one of Iris' projects. She had given them an exclusive to photograph Luc's much-talked-about Paradise restaurant for their January Interiors issue. Still, that didn't ensure a slam-dunk for this new pitch.

Nonetheless, Harmony sounded breathless with excitement as Iris walked her through the narrative about the handsome young Black artist whose warehouse had been torched, and the potential publicity of restoring the building as an artists' collaborative while, at the same time, highlighting a showcase of new eco-building construction.

"Great hook. Love the hook," Harmony kept repeating between deep drags on a cigarette.

When Iris got to the part about using Alex Harcon's new solar roof shingles, Harmony's enthusiasm bubbled over the phone line. "I've been dying to feature those damn tiles! I'll bet that Alex would fly in for a photo op shaking hands with the artist. How quickly do you think you can get this warehouse restored? Could it be ready for our September issue? You haven't pitched this to any other magazines, have you?"

Iris winked at Sheba. "Harmony, you're my first choice. If you're ready to commit to sponsoring the project, we're ready to commit exclusively to you."

# Chapter 10

Iris swiveled her hips to the beat of Beyoncé's "Sweet Dreams" playing through her earbuds as she watered the small herb garden on her kitchen windowsill. Suddenly she felt a pair of strong, gentle hands on her hips and a warm body swaying behind her. She reached back to squeeze a familiar left-hand ass cheek, then turned around.

"You knew it was me—right?" Luc leaned down to kiss her.

"Maybe," Iris murmured.

Sheba thumped her tail on the kitchen floor.

"You're in a good mood."

"I found a sponsor for Ash's renovation." She filled him in on the morning's progress as he moved away to unpack a loaded grocery bag. "And Milo agreed to take on the labor part because he's almost finished with work on his own house. He put that on hold to work on your restaurant."

"Which I'm grateful to the guy for doing. So s the magazine going to pay you for your time?"

"And Milo's! I was wondering how I was going to finagle

donated labor if it was a school project."

"I got me a smart woman. And now I'm gonna feed her." Luc dumped a carton of strawberries into a colander and ran them under cold tap water. "Ready for another experiment? I found some fresh-off-the-boat bluefin tuna and I want to serve it raw with a garnish I think might work."

"Oh, rats. I had my heart set on an Oscar Mayer fried bologna sandwich on Wonder Bread."

"Not in my kitchen." Taking out a razor-sharp knife, he cored and speed-chopped the strawberries. Next, he diced some tiny cucumbers into minuscule squares and tossed them together in a faint mist of vinaigrette. The garnish was sprinkled over two perfect little slabs of tuna. With the addition of a few shredded leaves of basil, freshly pinched off from the herb garden, their Instagram-worthy lunch was ready.

Iris set the table and took a bottle out of the fridge. "Will a Trebbiano do justice to your fancy crudo?"

"Perfetto." Luc brought the plates to the table.

They ate for a few minutes in reverential silence until Luc started in on his inevitable analysis. "Do you think the strawberries are too assertive? Or is it the cucumber that's too mild?"

They batted back and forth several possible adjustments to the recipe until Luc seemed satisfied. He jotted down some notes, then leaned back in his chair.

She caught Luc studying her. "What?" she asked.

His gaze drifted. "You're getting awfully invested in Raven's new boyfriend. He seems like a nice guy and I know he got a raw deal with the fire, but what happens when Raven gets bored, or he does, and they move on? Your dear goddaughter doesn't have a track record of sticking with one guy for very long."

Iris looked down thoughtfully into her empty wineglass. "She's only twenty and, chances are, she won't end up with Ash long-term. But I hope they hold it together for a while. At any rate, I want to help the kid. This arson business has me worried."

"Iris, please don't get mixed up in anything dangerous again." He rested his hand over his heart. "I couldn't take it."

"Ash is the one in the line of fire, so to speak. I'm wondering if someone is trying to scare him into selling his property." Iris bit her bottom lip. "Any chance your father's old partner would be able to get information about the investigation from the State Fire Marshal?"

"Ed? If the Fire Marshal is a Statie and not with the local cop shop, Ed wouldn't know anyone to pump."

"Oh, OK. Ash and I might try to talk with the guy who sold him the building. See if anyone else was interested in buying it."

"Be careful. Remember how your search for information last summer ended up?"

"As I recall, I got a dangerous criminal locked up."

"And almost got yourself killed."

# Chapter 11

On Tuesday afternoon, Ash drove up in his rust-eaten station wagon to Iris' new home, where she sat waiting on the front porch steps. When she slid into the sagging passenger seat, Ash was shaking his head, wide-eyed. "I can't believe you pulled this off. All these people are gonna donate free stuff to fix up my studio? This is a dream."

On the ride to Medford, almost shouting over the sound of the car's failing muffler, Iris filled Ash in on some of the details she'd pinned down that morning. The kid had never heard of Alex Harcon but was impressed by roof tiles that could supply energy for heating and cooling. "And they're clear glass? So, the roof will be like wall-to-wall skylights? Will that cause glare when the sun's overhead?"

"They're not totally clear because they're so thick. More like frosted," Iris explained. "And they have coils inside to absorb the solar energy."

Harmony had insisted on pitching the project herself to the charismatic mogul. Alex Harcon had immediately agreed to be the lead sponsor, saying that he'd been searching for ways to showcase his new product. According to Harmony, this was just the type of socially responsible project he wanted linked to his name.

Ash dropped her off in front of the building and gave her a key so she could get started measuring the space while he stopped by his mother's house to toss a load of laundry into the washer.

Iris' new Bosch laser measure made documenting the existing dimensions for a project a lot less tedious than using a measuring tape. She didn't completely trust its precision, but for the large expanses in a building like Ash's, it cut the time in half. She still measured the old-fashioned way for sill heights, the width of moldings and other smaller calibrations.

Forty minutes later, while squatting down to confirm the size of the massive wood columns holding up the roof trusses, Iris glimpsed a figure outside the windows. A young Black man calmly stared in at her through the glass, not moving, not smiling.

As Iris was wondering what to do next, she heard the loud grumbling of Ash's car approaching. The man outside the window turned his head, and they both watched the old station wagon rock to a stop. Ash got out and jogged toward the man, calling out to him. As Ash drew close, the two exchanged fist bumps and Ash led him over to the entrance.

Ash flung the door open. "Hey Iris, this is Jamal, Maggie's son."

Jamal smiled uncertainly and looked questioningly toward Ash.

"Iris is an architect, and she's helping me rebuild this place," Ash explained. "She's arranged for all these people to give us stuff to make it look good again. Better even."

Jamal looked around. "But it's all burned out. I saw the fire, man. It's gonna be too much work."

"It's OK. Iris knows how to fix up buildings. It will be my painting studio."

"You were already painting here," Jamal said. "And that other girl, too. The tall one with the funny hair."

"Yeah, that's my girlfriend. Iris is her godmother."

"Oh, OK." Jamal tilted his head as he looked at Iris, then Ash. He held up a green plastic disk on a chain. "I got my 90 day chip from NA, Ash. I've been straight for three months, see?"

"That's solid, man." Ash high-fived Jamal.

"I should go now. Tonight, I'm the head dishwasher at Mom's restaurant again."

After he left, Ash shook his head. "Guy's really lost it. It breaks my heart. We grew up together, our two families. His parents and my mom were friends at high school in Cambridge."

"Really? You didn't tell me you had Cambridge roots."

"Uh, huh. They went to Cambridge Rindge and Latin. But my Mom moved to Medford right after that."

"Luc went there. I wonder if he knows her. What's your

mother's name?"

"Angelique…it was Jackson back then. She's Angelique Burke now." He looked at the page on Iris' clipboard covered with her hieroglyphics written in every which direction. "You need to measure more?"

Iris' mind raced. *Ash's mother was Luc's gorgeous high-school girlfriend? She needed to think this through. Later, when she was alone.* She took a deep breath.

"All done." She stuffed the clipboard into her purse. "Let's go find Frank at the garage."

Frank's Auto Body Shop had seen better days. Or maybe not. Cardboard boxes, probably dragged over here when the warehouse was sold to Ash, were stacked up along the far wall of one bay. A Black man with close-cropped white hair wearing faded overalls was on his back twisting a wrench, a Cadillac precariously suspended above him. They headed over.

"Hey Frank," Ash said. "Speak to you for a minute?"

"Sure, Ashley. Give me a second to finish something here. Why don't you wait in my office? Help yourselves to coffee."

Ash and Iris squeezed into a tiny room whose grimy plate-glass window overlooked the garage interior. The smell of burned coffee emanated from the almost-empty carafe on a Mr. Coffee machine set on a side table. Neither of them was interested in the tarry residue. Most of the room was taken up by a metal desk covered with piles of paperwork and an ancient desktop computer. A lone calendar from Champion spark plugs, four years out of date, adorned the wall. Ash gestured for

Iris to take the one uncomfortable-looking guest chair while he perched on the windowsill. She sank into it, adjusting herself to its random springs, her mind still pre-occupied with Ash's bombshell about his mother.

Frank entered, wiping his hands on a grimy rag, then patted the younger man's shoulder. "Terrible thing, that fire, Ashley."

Ash stepped aside to let Frank move to his desk chair. "This is Iris Reid, an architect who was with me on Saturday night. She's going to help me renovate the building."

Frank gave her a nod. "Best of luck, ma'am."

Ash asked, "Did you see anyone hanging around that night before the fire?"

"It was around supper time?"

"Right, between 6:30 and 7."

"Naw, I'd closed up shop by then. But they could've been in the woods on the other side," Frank pointed out. "Some guy threw a Molotov cocktail, right?"

Ash glanced at Iris. "The Fire Marshall didn't tell me that," he said.

"That's the word on the street, anyway. June Pitt with the big mouth is married to the fireman who found some pieces of it on the floor, glass and such. Someone with a good arm could have lobbed it up onto the roof. They say that's where the fire started. Punks could've been hiding in the woods."

"Did you hear any guesses who did it or why? Does someone have it in for me?"

Frank shook his head. "No, no. My guess is random

mischief. Any bored fool can make a one of those fire bombs these days. There're instructions on the internet. But I've been wondering why now? Warehouse has been sitting there practically empty all these years, and now that you want to put it to good use, some useless lowlifes try to torch it? It's just damn bad luck, excuse my language. I'm so sorry, son."

A vein throbbed at Ash's temple. "I'm gonna salvage it, Frank. Iris is going to help me. This fire won't stop my plans."

Frank eyed Iris approvingly. "I'm real glad to hear that."

Iris tried to focus on why they were there. "Frank, you mentioned the timing of the fire. Had anyone besides Ash ever shown any interest in buying that property?"

Frank rubbed his chin and shook his head. "No, I can't think of anyone else who ever asked me about it."

# Chapter 12

On her ride home, while her Uber battled rush-hour traffic, Iris mulled over this new knowledge about what had happened to Luc's old girlfriend. She didn't know *why* the woman had moved to Medford, she just knew *where* she'd gone and *when*. She wondered if Luc had ever learned the why, the where, or the when. Should she even bring up the subject?

By the time Iris climbed the stairs to the apartment, Luc was already in the kitchen getting dinner ready, Sheba at his feet. Iris leaned down to scratch her dog behind the ears, then stood up to lean in and kiss Luc.

"I get second billing after the dog?" He pulled her close. "Hmm… we'll have to give you a reason to change my standing."

"Age before beauty. Sheba is fifty-six in dog years."

"So, what have you been up to this afternoon?"

"I measured Ash's warehouse and then the two of us talked with the garage owner who sold him the place. Seems that there was no shadowy developer-behind-the-scenes who was angry that Ash snatched the warehouse out from under him or anything like that. Still, I'm not ready to throw out my theory about hot-property greed being the motive for the fire, not just yet. The Green Line trolley is supposed to get extended out to Medford soon and all the land anywhere near the new station will skyrocket in value."

"Follow the money, as they say." Luc handed her a plastic spinner of washed greens. "You want to make the salad while you tell me more about it? I'll pour you a glass of wine."

Iris washed her hands and pulled a wooden bowl out of a drawer. She willed her voice to sound light. "Here's a coincidence for you. Ash told me that his mother went to Cambridge Rindge and Latin."

"Try this." Luc handed her a glass of Rosso de Montepulciano. "What's her name?"

Iris took a sip. "Ooh, I like this one." She pretended to think for a minute. "It started with an 'A'. Wait, Angelique, that's it."

Luc set the bottle down a little too abruptly and asked, "Angelique Jackson?"

"You knew her? I saw a portrait that Ash painted of her."

He turned on the range hood fan and threw a steak from a nearby plate onto the range's hot center grill. "Yeah…you said she's Ash's mother?"

"Uh, huh."

"And Ash grew up in Medford?" Luc asked, still facing away. He poked at the steak with a fork. Maybe sooner than it needed.

Iris tossed the salad. "Right, I think he said he's lived there all his life. Angelique must have been pretty young when she had him."

"I just have this ribeye and a salad for tonight." Luc flipped the steak over. "Is that going to be enough for you?"

Luc barely touched his dinner. His face seemed distant and clouded by what Iris imagined were thoughts about Angelique. As soon as Iris finished her last bite, he stood up. "I need to go downstairs and get a few things ready for tomorrow." He brought his plate to the kitchen and disappeared down the stairs.

She loaded the dishwasher, then called to Sheba for "walkies". The dog immediately leapt to her feet from her prone position on the kitchen floor.

Outside in the cold, Iris wrapped her parka closer around her body and leaned against the exterior wall of the restaurant's kitchen. A window nearby was slightly open. As she waited interminably for Sheba to find a choice spot to circle, she could hear Luc talking on the phone.

"You're damn straight I'm upset. You know what I went through, thinking she was dead. And she's been two fucking towns away this whole time." His voice broke. "I've gotta go."

So he hadn't known. Who was he talking to? Iris felt in her pocket for her own phone and pressed the speed-dial for Ellie.

"Hi. It's me. Can we meet for breakfast tomorrow?"

# Chapter 13

Early the next morning, Luc lay blinking in the dim light, fighting the impulse to tilt back into sleep. Then, taking a deep breath, he made the effort—rolled out of bed. He threw on a pair of ripped jeans and an old sweater, then slipped out of the apartment before Iris woke up. A thin layer of frost covered the van.

He drove the familiar route past his mother's house near Inman Square and on for two more blocks. Angel's old apartment, a run-down brick mid-rise, caught the weak morning sun. Luc sat in his van, double-parked, staring at the building—knowing that she and her mother had left two decades before. He looked up at the windows of her old living room, the scene of many of their trysts. Iris couldn't have known that her information from the previous night had hit him with the force of a massive hand squeezing his heart.

Luc could remember the thrill he felt as he'd watched Angel cross the school lawn to meet him after their high school classes. They'd saunter down Cambridge Street hand-in-hand to this very building. Luc's family's tidy Cape-style home was closer to school, but it had a vigilant mother in residence, whereas Angel's mother worked and was never home before dinner. After a month of superhuman restraint on Luc's part, their attention to homework would get interrupted by passionate interludes on the living room sofa. Not that Luc had had anything to compare it to, but their bodies seemed to fit together perfectly in every respect. Their minds too. They'd told each other everything. They made each other mix tapes with their favorite music and shared their dreams for the future. He'd believed that they were soul mates, destined to be together. *He had never really let her go.*

Luc rested his forehead against the steering wheel. Talking to Declan the previous night had not made him feel any better. His friend had been as mystified as he'd been that Angelique had stayed so close. It was not until later that night, while lying in bed wide-awake, that he had worked out a possible explanation for Angel's disappearing act. Now he needed to test that idea.

He slid out his phone, Googled an address, and slid the van into gear. He'd never been to this house in Cambridgeport before. It belonged to Shania Johnson, a friend of Angel's back in high school. He navigated through Central Square's complicated traffic and located the street. After several passes around Shania's block, he eased into a parking space and sat collecting his thoughts. Angel had hung out with a wild crowd of her own age before she'd met Luc. She'd remained close with them when she wasn't spending time with him. Luc had checked with several of those friends right after Angel's disappearance, but no one had heard from her. It hadn't occurred to him to check again later to see if she'd gotten back in touch.

The woman who answered the door recognized him immediately. "Well, if it isn't the hottest chef in America on my doorstep! Cormier, you look like shit. Come on in." Shania looked like what she was, a woman pushing forty who'd smoked cigarettes for most of her life, but she dressed like a teenager in skinny jeans and red Chuck Taylor high tops. She still wore her jet black hair in tight cornrows.

She led him into her messy living room, littered with an overflowing ashtray, parts of kids' soccer uniforms, and plastic super hero action figures. "What'd the magazine do to get that cover—photo shop you onto some movie star?"

Luc gave her a hug, then self-consciously rubbed the day's worth of stubble on his angled jaw. "Sounds like you've got my cover pinned up somewhere. How're you doing, Shan? Looks like you've got some kids."

"Yeah, a couple of overgrown rug rats. They just left for school, so I get a chance to hear myself think."

Luc forced up a tired smile. "I came to ask you about Angel."

"Yeah, I figured." Shania gave him a look of concern and pity. "Have a seat. You want anything? Coffee?"

Luc pushed aside some tiny pink leggings from the sofa and

perched on the edge. "I'm good. So, have you talked to her?"

Shania sat across from him and examined her elaborately detailed nails. "All those years ago when you called and asked me that, I told you the truth. She'd disappeared on me the same way she did on you." She picked up a small, glittery Beyoncé sweatshirt off the floor and smoothed it on her lap. "I didn't hear a peep from her for maybe ten, twelve years. Then I got a phone call. She came by and we talked." Shania studied Luc's face. "Did you know she had a kid?"

"I just found out, but not from her. I haven't talked with her yet. She's volunteering at a clinic in Haiti until Christmas."

"Yeah, well, she asked about you. What I knew. I said I heard you were living in Rome and were married to some Italian girl. She didn't want to talk about you after that. She'd gotten married too. He sounded like a nice guy. But she was alone with her son for a couple of years before she met him. I guess it was tough going for a while. She never said why she didn't go off to California like she planned."

"Yeah, her son." Luc let the words hang in the air for a minute. "I need to ask you—is he my kid?"

Shania reached for a pack of cigarettes on the coffee table and slid one out. She lit it, took a deep practiced drag, then blew a stream of smoke sideways. "Angelique wouldn't say. Showed me a picture though, and he sure looks a helluva lot like the two of you combined."

# Chapter 14

Sitting in her friend's kitchen, Iris waited until Ellie had poured them both big steaming cups of coffee before she cut to the chase. "It turns out that Ash's mother was Luc's long-ago high-school girlfriend."

Ellie's mouth fell open. "Excuse me?"

"Mary dropped off a box of Luc's childhood and school things from his mother's house two weeks ago and, obviously, I had to look through it."

"Obviously."

Iris reached into her purse for her cell phone and opened her photos to the one showing teen-aged Luc and Angelique, arms intertwined. She passed it across the table to Ellie.

"Wait—how did you get this picture?"

Iris studied the surface of her coffee. "I took shots of some photos I found in Luc's box."

Ellie looked at her friend, then back at the phone. "This is her? Oh, shit. She's drop-dead. And look at Luc," Ellie said in a high-pitched voice. "He's *so young and adorable* with those sideburns."

Iris raised her eyebrows.

Ellie continued. "Sorry. You know you're beautiful too. But how can you be so sure that this is Ash's mother?"

"Ash mentioned yesterday that she'd gone to Cambridge Rindge and Latin, so I asked him what her name was. I knew that Angelique Jackson was Luc's girlfriend because a bunch of letters he had written to her were also in the box."

"You read his letters?"

"No," Iris said, indignantly. "They were sealed."

"He hadn't sent them?"

"The letters were sent, but they were all returned, unopened. She was a year ahead of him in school and supposedly went off to Berkeley for college. But I think, once she left, she just ghosted him."

"How could any woman ghost that adorable young Luc?"

"And I get the impression he was devastated by her disappearing from his life," Iris said.

"Did you talk to him about it?"

"I couldn't very well tell him that I'd gone through his personal stuff, but I mentioned the business about Ash saying that his mother went to Luc's high school and asked if he'd known her. When I mentioned her name, I could tell right away that he was shaken. Luc admitted that he knew her, but acted like it was no big deal. Then he was practically catatonic all through dinner, and afterward I heard him talking on the phone with someone about how upset he was that she'd been living close by all along."

Ellie picked up a piece of buttered toast from her plate, bit off a piece and chewed thoughtfully. "I can't believe this is Ash's mother we're talking about. The noble nurse who's gone off to Haiti to save lives? She broke Luc's heart? The poor guy. And you don't think they've seen each other since high school?"

"It doesn't sound like it. I wonder what will happen when she gets back to town in a couple of weeks. You saw the photo. They clearly adored each other."

"Yeah, a couple of decades ago, a couple of teenagers." Ellie rolled her eyes. "So Angelique moved on, got married, had a kid. And Luc moved on too. He's with you now and he adores *you*."

Iris stared down at her uneaten toast. "What if they want to be together again? Ash told me that his father died last year, so Angelique's a free woman. You hear all the time about people going to their twentieth high school reunions and reigniting old romances."

"You don't know what it would be like if they ever do meet up again. It might not even happen."

"Now I wish I hadn't volunteered to do this project with Ash. He's a nice kid, but at this point I'd love to get some distance from him."

"Then again, if Raven and Ash stay together, we'll all be one big, happy family."

Iris narrowed her eyes at her friend.

# Chapter 15

When Iris returned to their apartment around nine that morning, she peeked into the ground-floor restaurant kitchen on the way up. Luc wasn't there, and his van was missing from the small parking lot. He had been gone when she'd woken up that morning as well. Usually he liked nothing more than to lounge in bed with her, savoring the fact that the restaurant didn't require his attention until the afternoon.

Iris retreated to her home office to focus on her own work. She settled down in front of her computer and spent the next hour reading her scrawled dimensions off a sheet of paper and plugging them into a BIM program. Locating the wood columns was particularly tricky since they were of random sizes and not evenly spaced. But slowly, an accurate floor plan of the warehouse as it existed appeared on the screen.

After the plan view was blocked out, she added in the vertical measurements for the windows and doors. Four exterior elevations, two-dimensional representations of the building's walls, eventually appeared: north, east, south, and west; the street frontage, back wall and the two smaller ends. She studied them, trying to decide if any of their proportions needed some sympathetic design intervention. She played back-and-forth with more controls and considered the building in 3-D from different angles. Finally, she returned to the two-dimensional view of the floor plan and sent the image to the plotter.

While the drawing was printing out, she scooted on her chair over toward the hall to listen for sounds of anyone else moving around. Nothing, except for far-off traffic sounds from Mass Ave. The time on her phone read eleven-thirty. She stood up and stretched.

She collected the 11" x 17" sheet of translucent mylar film of the floor plan and taped it to her drafting table, lining up the building's long walls with the parallel edge of her Mayline. The specifications and photographs of the individual items that the many companies had pledged to provide lay in separate piles on the bare wood floor. She stuck these up on the walls surrounding her desk with drafting tape.

Now she was ready to sketch. After retrieving a small roll of cream-colored tracing paper from a floor-to-ceiling bookshelf that lined one wall of her office, she tore off a section against the edge of her triangular architect's ruler and laid it over the CAD drawing.

This was Iris' favorite part of a project—the design. Each project required a different balance between the creative possibilities versus the practical solutions to the puzzle. Here, four artists' live-work spaces needed to be integrated with the mechanical and structural requirements of the building. Seeing space three-dimensionally had always felt intuitive to her. When proportions were off and rooms were awkwardly arranged, red sensors went off in her brain.

She opened up the technical specifications for the solar roof shingles and read through a long set of detailed requirements for their structural support. There would need to be an intermediate substructure between the roof trusses and the special shingles. Ordinarily there were roof joists every sixteen inches and a layer of plywood sheathing, not to mention waterproofing and shingles on top. But that system would block the translucency of the high-tech glass tiles. So, Harcon's designers had crafted a 3-D membrane out of a polymer to be used for support instead. This would look very cool but sounded complicated to build.

Then Iris noticed a hand-written scrawl in the margin of the Harcon specs: "We will supply this. Please have Architect co-ordinate with me personally." It was initialed: A. H.

Iris took a deep breath and released it. Alex Harcon himself had written that note. She would be exchanging notes with the visionary genius himself. That was reason enough to do this project.

She sat back in her chair, smiling, and almost missed the sound of tentative footsteps coming up the staircase.

Iris went out to the hall to meet Luc. As he climbed the last few steps into their apartment, he met her eyes. "Look, there's something I've got to tell you." He cleared his throat. "Can we sit down in the living room?"

Iris followed him, Sheba at her heels, dreading what he might have to say.

Luc sat on the edge of the sofa, his hands dangling between his knees. "You asked me last night if I knew Angelique Jackson in high school. I should've told you, she was my girlfriend when I was a junior and she was a senior."

His voice was tight, his words clipped.

"Was it a bad break-up?"

"We didn't exactly break-up. She was supposed to fly to California to start college out there. She didn't want me to drive her to the airport, so we said our goodbyes the night before. And that was the last time I ever saw or heard from her. We'd been planning on dating long-distance during that year before I graduated and could go out to join her, but she just dropped off the radar."

"She didn't even write you a 'dear John' letter?"

"Nothing."

"Wow. I'm so sorry."

"To make matters worse, my father was killed at the end of that summer. It was a rough time all around. So, hearing her name brings up a lot of shitty memories."

Iris moved next to him on the sofa. "Oh, babe…Thanks for telling me."

"Learning that she lives a few towns away, that she's been around here the whole time after high school is really flipping me out."

"Yeah, I'll bet."

His hand trailed down her arm. "I'm going to need to meet with Angel when she gets back. Get it resolved once and for all. You don't mind, do you?"

More than a few responses went through her mind. She wished he'd stop calling her "Angel" for one thing. "No, I understand."

"She's in Haiti now—isn't she? I remember Ash telling me that his grandmother lived there."

"She's a nurse and is volunteering at a clinic down there. Ash said she's due back sometime before Christmas."

Luc leaned closer. "This isn't going to change anything between you and me. We're good—right?"

# Chapter 16

I ris spent the rest of the day trying to lose herself in the design of Ash's warehouse, all the while shadowed by a sense of foreboding at the thought of Luc and Angelique's reunion.

Back at her drafting table, she sketched out an efficient circulation scheme and found a logical spot to stash the giant battery necessary to store the power from the roof tiles. This would provide electricity for heating, air conditioning, and even power for the kitchen ranges. Next to the battery, she left enough space for a small back-up generator. The floors would remain concrete, with floor drains added for practical clean-up. Green-Steel was contributing all new and very cool-looking windows with Low-E glass. Iris used the donated reclaimed wood as vertical siding for the partition walls. The locations and layouts for four kitchenettes and bathrooms were clustered in the building's core, and the basic layout was set.

She completed the floor plan, the interior and exterior elevations, drew kitchen elevations at half-inch scale, and typed up a window and door schedule. She'd incorporated all of the contributed items, checking their specifications to make sure they all meshed together. The structural drawings would have to wait until she talked with Alex Harcon about the necessary roof substructure. Come to think of it, Milo might need to be at that meeting as well. And they'd have to meet soon because Milo would require final structural drawings in order to apply for the building permit. Would Harcon fly her and Milo out to California on one of his private planes, or would the great man himself jet out east to Massachusetts? The whole set-up felt unreal.

While the drawings were working their way through the printer, Iris texted Ash to set up a meeting right after his classes were done to get his approval and sign-off. He was the client, after all. He texted right back, saying that he could be at her apartment at five.

This project was moving at lightning speed, but if construction was going to be completed and photographed in time for *Architecture Now!*'s September issue, they'd have to start construction by the first of the year. Manufacturing the polymer sub-roof framing would need to go into production soon after that. Iris found the prospect of fast-tracking a construction job to be exhilarating, like walking a tightrope without a net. There was no margin for error. She'd always been a quick designer. Two decades of experience gave her the ability to anticipate all the interrelated steps in the construction process and the complex ways in which they needed to fit together.

A compressed schedule also relied on the nimbleness and organization of the General Contractor. During Luc's restaurant renovation Milo, though still in his early thirties, had proven that he had the knowledge and leadership skills to manage his crew effectively. Iris also appreciated that he was easygoing and had none of the typical Contractor's ego problems when working with a female architect.

At a quarter to five, Iris tidied up the open-plan area of her loft and spread out the dozen drawings on the dining room table, which served double-duty as a conference table. She also set out a small batch of cheeses and crackers on an oval platter. After all, Ash was more than a mere client. He was her goddaughter's boyfriend. And that brought her thoughts immediately back to Luc. How would he relate to Ash now that he knew that the young man was the son of his first love?

At this hour, Luc was downstairs, helping to prepare dinner for his wait staff and drilling them on the evening's specials. Would he be fantasizing about returning to Angelique instead of staying with Iris? She had thrown her fate in with his, sold her family home, sunk all her savings into this building, and moved in to share her life with him. Now he wanted to meet up with an ex-lover in order to find "closure," or worse, to maybe re-ignite a long-abandoned love affair.

She heard the unmistakable coughing sounds of Ash's car

pulling alongside the building and into the rear parking lot. She buzzed him in and he climbed up two stairs at a time. "You have drawings already? Things are sure moving fast."

Iris took Ash's parka, hung it up, and directed him toward the black line prints spread out like an offering on the oversized table. He stood, gazing down at them and dragging his fingers over the title block which read: 20 Harvard Avenue, Medford, MA, Owner: Ashley Burke. He inspected the exterior elevations with the glass roof tiles carefully drawn in and the interior with its vertical wood siding. "So cool," he murmured. "I can't believe this will be my studio."

Ash's down-turned profile was at the edge of Iris' vision. She couldn't help herself looking for traces of his beautiful mother.

# Chapter 17

When Iris drove up to the warehouse the next morning, Milo was already there, straddling his blue motorcycle, his helmet strap looped over his left arm. When he saw her, he shoved his phone back into his pocket and headed her way.

She stepped out of the car and called out to him, "Can you give me a hand with these saw-horses?"

Milo raised his eyebrows. "I thought *I* was supposed to bring the construction materials."

Iris responded by dragging a half sheet of plywood out of the cargo area of her Jeep. "I want to set up a table so I can show you the drawings."

"You just got a sponsor for this project a few days ago and you've already produced drawings?"

"It's a tight deadline." Iris unlocked the warehouse door and lugged the 4 x 4 sheet of plywood to the center of the open room while Milo followed with a sawhorse under each arm. He set up a sturdy makeshift desk, then looked around at the battle-scarred space. Plywood covered the jagged gash in the roof and the brick walls were still streaked with soot. Nevertheless, it looked far better than it had on Sunday.

"How did you get the smoke smell out so fast?" Milo asked. "I can actually breathe in here today."

"I called in some post-fire specialists and they stripped everything down to the brick. Four industrial fans have been pulling fresh air through the space for three days." Iris reached into her bag. "I wanted you to check out these drawings and to look at my ideas for the space. See if I've missed anything."

Milo's eyes widened as he watched her unfurl an impressive roll of prints. He flipped through them. "You even did a window and door schedule? Do you ever sleep?"

"Just about everything is donated, so the specs were all a given. I just had to organize the space and plug in everything to scale."

Iris walked him through the floor plans and elevations, explaining all the special characteristics about the green products they'd be using.

"These are some really expensive windows. Green-steel is giving them to the project for free? Maybe I should become an artist."

These companies and the magazine are doing this for the publicity. The project will get a lot of attention. You and I will also get some good P.R. out of this."

"I'll alert my marketing team."

Iris rolled her eyes. "I'll still need to get you the structural drawings."

"I noticed that."

"I can draw up wall sections, but Alex Harcon's people will need to design and provide the superstructure to support the special roof tiles."

Milo tilted his head. "What do you mean 'provide'? Are they installing it?"

"I'm not sure. I need to talk with him soon to clarify that. When you put together your cost numbers, just leave that labor column blank for now. Harcon will need to co-ordinate that step with you."

"Any chance I'll get to meet Alex Harcon in person to shoot the breeze about the fine points of construction?" he asked.

"We'll see. He'll probably fob us off onto one of his structural engineers." Iris said. "How long is the City of Medford taking to issue permits these days?"

"Good question. I'll check." He leaned against one of the large wood columns and jotted down some notes on his phone. He thought for a minute. "Let's go outside. I want to see where I can put a dumpster or two."

Iris led him out the back door to a small parking lot which faced a wooded area. She pointed out the vestiges of several old brick kilns attached to the exterior wall. "This building was part of a brick-making factory in the eighteenth and nineteenth centuries."

Milo walked around the perimeter of the large lot, looking at everything. He stopped in front of a large brick cylinder sticking up about four feet out of the ground. "What's this thing?"

Iris looked at it and tried to remember. "I think Ash said it was the base of an old chimney for one of the kilns."

Milo peered in over the edge. "I wonder how deep it goes?"

Iris looked in as well. It was filled with leaves, dirty water and muck.

Milo reached in and gingerly pulled out a handful of wet leaves. "This could become a retention pond for rainwater. I'd imagine that four artists will use a lot of grey water to clean their brushes."

"Great idea," Iris agreed. "I'll look into the requirements. It will need some kind of pump to circulate the water. We wouldn't want mosquitos breeding in there." She squinted and raised a hand to shade her eyes from the sun, catching a reflection of light coming from the adjacent woods behind Milo's head.

Iris held still and murmured, "Don't turn around. Someone is watching us." She eased her phone out of her pocket and pretended to take a few photos of the chimney while including the section of the woods where the telltale light had come from.

Milo froze. "Curious neighbor?" He shifted his weight to the balls of his feet.

She could make out a crouched figure just visible behind a tree. She whispered, "He's watching us through binoculars. Given the case of arson last Saturday, I'd sure like to talk to this guy. Twenty yards away. Just over your right shoulder."

Milo spun around and they both sprinted in that direction.

# Chapter 18

T en minutes later, Iris and Milo were both bent over at the waist, hands on their knees, panting hard.

"That guy must be a rabbit," Milo said, "the way he ran."

"Where'd he go?" Iris dropped onto the grass alongside a church parking lot. "He just vanished."

Milo collapsed down beside her. He took several deep breaths. "I don't like this. First, someone sets the building on fire. Then, some guy is spying on the property. Is there gonna be trouble on this project? Are my guys gonna have to wear bulletproof vests above their tool belts?"

"I don't know what's going on," Iris admitted. "I wonder if Ash paid some neighborhood kid to watch things and he got spooked when we started after him."

Milo gave her a skeptical look.

"I'll text him and ask." Iris fished out her smartphone and thumbed out a message. She almost immediately got Ash's response: *no, why?*

Milo pulled at his lower lip. "I'm responsible for these guys and I don't want to put them in danger. This sounds like a cool project and I'd love to schmooze with Alex Harcon, but…"

"Wait. Don't go backing out on me. Let me talk with the Arson investigator and see what they've turned up. We'll get this sorted out before construction starts, OK?"

"Fine, but I really need to get some reassurance soon, before I pull the building permit with my name on it."

Iris arrived home half an hour later, pulling her Jeep into her parking spot next to Luc's van, but as she climbed the stairs and walked through the empty apartment to her home office, only Sheba greeted her. Getting an appointment with Phil Weaver, the State Fire Marshall, was easier than she'd expected. He said he could fit her in if she came by his office within the next hour. Iris fixed herself a quick lunch and changed out of her comfortable jeans into a severely tailored navy suit—something she often wore for initial client meetings to look her most professional.

Weaver's office was in the State Police Headquarters in Brighton, a squat shoebox of a building along the Charles River, a long way from downtown. The fresh-faced State policeman with a serious attitude behind the reception desk kept her waiting for forty minutes. The Staties passing in and out, all male and all white, made no attempt to conceal their efforts to check her out. She tried to ignore them and spent her time going through the morning's photographs on her phone until Weaver finally appeared. He gave her a cursory handshake and led her back to his windowless office. The room and its furnishings cried out drab, government-issued, soulless.

Up close, Iris could see that the man was probably no older than fifty, despite his snow-white crewcut. Today, he was dressed in a gray sports jacket instead of his official windbreaker, but he still wore the same suspicious expression. Weaver motioned her over to a straight back wooden chair and settled himself behind his desk. "What can I do for you, Ms. Reid?"

"I was out at 20 Harvard Avenue in Medford this morning with the contractor who's going to renovate that warehouse, the one where the fire was last week. We were in the back parking lot when I noticed someone in the woods watching us through binoculars. We chased him, but he got away." Iris passed her phone to him showing a blown-up but blurry photo of a crouching figure. "Did you assign anyone to watch the property?"

Weaver studied the image. "We're not doing any surveillance at this point." He punched a few buttons on her phone. "Hope you don't mind—I've forwarded this to our tech lab to see if they can sharpen it up. Can you give me a description of the guy?"

Iris closed her eyes and thought. "He had on a light-colored hoodie so his face was in shadow but I'm pretty sure it was a male from his shape and the way he moved. He ran fast. The pants were dark, I think. He had a medium build and was medium height, an inch or two under six feet. That's all I could see."

Weaver jotted this down on a pad of paper. "Race? Hair color?"

Iris shook her head. "I couldn't tell."

"Any idea why someone would have an interest in this property?"

"I was going to ask you that. My building contractor is concerned about whether this site is going to be safe for his workers. Have you made any progress in tracking down the arsonist?"

"I can't discuss that with the general public."

"I'm not the general public. I'm a professional who needs to have construction workers in that building soon and I need to be sure it's safe. Isn't safety a concern of the State Police?"

Weaver glanced not-so-discretely at his watch.

"Have there been other cases where a building's been broken into, the sprinkler system disabled, and an arsonist has thrown a Molotov cocktail up onto the roof? Has that M.O. shown up in the arson databank?"

Weaver's eyes narrowed. "How did you know how the fire was started?"

"Everyone in Medford seems to know. And I saw the smashed sprinkler controls myself."

"Thank you for telling me about this person watching the site today." Weaver stood up. "We'll be in touch if we have any more information that we can share with you."

# Chapter 19

On her drive home, Iris wondered how she could convince Milo that the construction site would be safe and incident-free. If today's spy in the woods was indeed the firebug, then he was still on the loose. And even if Weaver had some leads on the guy, he wasn't going to tell her if he was anywhere close to making an arrest.

Maybe this project *was* too dangerous, at least right now. Maybe *she* shouldn't be working on it until the arsonist was caught.

As Iris trudged back up the steps to her apartment, she weighed the stakes: she'd already completed the design; she'd convinced numerous high-profile sponsors to donate newsworthy products; and this showcase might be an important influence on the building industry, especially with its debut of the revolutionary Harcon solar roof tiles.

When she reached the top of the staircase, she saw Luc standing in the open-plan kitchen, staring vacantly into the open refrigerator. Blond stubble covered his cheeks.

He closed the door and looked over at her. "Hi."

"Hi. Where have you been? You were gone again when I woke up."

"Sorry." He looked like he hadn't slept. "I've been out walking."

Iris approached Luc and gave him a hug. "Have you had lunch? Want me to fix you something?"

"I'm not really hungry. I've been drinking too much coffee. You got a minute? There's something I've been thinking about."

At that moment, Iris' cell phone rang. She glanced at the caller ID, planning to ignore it, when she noticed that Alex Harcon was on the line. Still, she hesitated, ran a hand down Luc's arm, and said, "I should really take this. Can we talk later?"

He nodded. She headed to her office, swiping up on the screen to answer the call. She sat down at her drafting table. "Alex, it's Iris Reid here. I'm so excited to be working with you. Did you get the PDFs of the drawings I sent last night?"

"Yes, and I'm impressed that you've put together this package so quickly." His voice was steady, low and authoritative. "I understand that the magazine has us on a tight schedule and thought I should get you together with my team to go over the roof specifications. My head engineer would like to fly out to take his own measurements for the roof assembly." Harcon paused. "The design for the sub-roof was actually invented in your city by the Oxman team at the MIT Media

Lab. It's made from a new polymer derived from shrimp shells."

"You're kidding?"

"No, Professor Oxman has been working on this for years. She got her first batch of shrimp shells from the restaurant, Legal Sea Foods." Harcon sounded like an excited kid. "The Lab crafted the 3-D-printed membrane from Jumbo crustacean polymers, fruit pectin and cellulose from old newspapers."

"That's brilliant."

"It's also completely biodegradable, once the UV-stabilized coating is neutralized. This is the future, Ms. Reid."

"I'll be honored to be the first to use it."

"It's critical that we install the system in a very specific way. I'd like to have my own people install it. That won't be a problem with the contractor, will it?"

Iris paused, remembering Milo's reservations about attaching himself to the project.

Harcon seemed to pick up on her hesitation. "You mentioned in your email that you had a building contractor involved with whom you've worked before, and that he was ready to start right away. Is there a problem?"

Iris decided to lay her cards on the table. Perhaps this influential man could help. "Harmony told you, didn't she, that someone tried to burn down this warehouse last week? We don't know the arsonist's motive and he or she has yet to be caught. Today, I was walking the site with the contractor and we saw someone watching us through binoculars from some nearby woods. Now, Milo, the contractor, is reluctant to proceed until the culprit is found and arrested."

Harcon asked a few more pertinent questions. There was silence for a minute before he asked, "Is there another contractor you could use?"

"I doubt that anyone else could start right away. And I'm not sure if, ethically, I should withhold information about possible danger from anyone who might be exposed to it, working on the site."

"Hmm. You're probably right." Harcon paused a beat. "The bottom line seems to be that the building site needs to be secured. We don't necessarily need to have the arsonist caught. If I had my California security team put cameras and sensors around the property, they could monitor the feeds 24/7 from here. They do that anyway for my other buildings. That way, if they see anyone suspicious, they'd be tied in to the local police department and could have the police on site right away. Do you think this might convince your Mr. Milo to move ahead?"

# Chapter 20

Luc sat hunched over his iPad in the quiet restaurant kitchen, trying to focus on a new menu for the winter season. Should he substitute Acadian redfish for the sea bass in the fish soup? Would mint and Sichuan peppercorns be too overpowering for the fluke crudo? He stared out the window at the last of the dead leaves lying in the corners of their small, fenced-in yard. He'd meant to rake and bag them last weekend. Iris had been doing most of the heavy lifting lately, even cooking most of the recent Thanksgiving meal.

It was just as well that Iris' phone call had kept him from blurting out what had been haunting him ever since his visit with Shania—that he might be Ash's father. He should make sure before he introduced this major complication into his relationship with her. Was it really possible that Angel had been pregnant with his child when she disappeared? Had she just learned about it and acted on some misguided, noble bullshit—like he was too young to be a father at seventeen, that it would ruin his life? That would provide the explanation he'd been unable to come up with over the years. But why would she have kept him from even knowing that a child existed? How could she have done that to him? How could she have done that to their son? Then, however many years later, did Shania telling Angel that he was living in Italy, married, push her to abandon the idea of ever contacting him?

That old raw wound of abandonment burned hot, again. Angel had left him to circle this emotional black hole alone. His father's murder had been in all the papers at the time. A cop killing was big news, so she wouldn't have missed it. But she'd chosen to vanish and leave him to mourn by himself. She'd chosen to raise their child alone. And based on what Iris had discovered, Angel had had plenty of opportunity to contact him at any point if she had wanted to. She hadn't gone off to California. She'd just moved two towns away.

Luc had missed everything—seeing his child's first appearance into the world, holding him, hearing Ash's first words, reading to him, teaching him stuff like how to play Ultimate Frisbee. Luc was sure that he would've been a good father, maybe even a good husband.

But now, perhaps, fate had brought his son back into his life. Why hadn't he noticed or felt something when they'd been introduced ten days before? Why hadn't his family sensed the presence of their blood relative at the Thanksgiving table?

Should he try to talk to Ash himself?

Luc raked his hands through his hair. No, he could still be wrong. He didn't know exactly when Ash had been born. It was possible that Angelique had left him to start a new life and gotten pregnant by some other guy. His stomach turned to ice at that possibility, even now, twenty years later.

He would arrange to talk with Angelique when she returned from Haiti.

But how could he stand to wait another two weeks for answers? *How could he wait that long to see her face again?*

# Chapter 21

Ash removed his earbuds and stuck them into his T-shirt pocket, the loud Thelonious Monk track he'd been listening to still audible. He stood back from the easel to study his latest painting. Yeah, this one was definitely working. He'd been expanding on the style of his self-portrait, mixing abstract and figurative shapes, using a mix of personal and social themes. He'd interwoven images from his own memories with questions about social and economic identity. Raven had dubbed it his "signature vibe".

This painting showed five brightly dressed figures he'd remembered seeing two years before dancing and making music on a beach in Haiti. You could barely make out their forms and instruments, though. It was more the essence of their movements that expressed the feeling he'd remembered from that afternoon. He'd added an ominous dark blue shadow, a wall almost, rising from the sand along one side of the canvas. Should he paint something lighter on top of the blue? An allusion to something more optimistic?

A faint buzzing broke into his thoughts. He looked over at his phone resting nearby on a high windowsill, but it wasn't a call. Raven usually texted him when she knew he was working. The time read a few minutes after midnight. The doorbell? It buzzed again. Ash jogged up the rickety basement steps and could see an outline of a head through the front door's frosted glass pane. He approached cautiously. "Who is it?"

"Medford Police," a female voice called. "Are you Ashley Burke, the owner of 20 Harvard Avenue?"

Ash opened the door a crack. "I'm Ash. Can I see your identification?"

A short young female cop and her tall male colleague, both in uniform, passed him their ID badges.

Ash checked them both and handed them back. "What do you want to talk to me about at this hour?"

"There's a fire on your property," the woman said.

Ash groaned. "Not again!"

"We'd like to drive you there, ask you some questions on the way."

Ash looked over at the squad car standing at the curb. "I'm not sitting in the back of a police car. I'll meet you there." He grabbed his coat from the hall closet, locked the door and set off at a run.

In the few minutes that it took him to cover the short blocks, he considered that he was dressed in ripped, paint-splattered jeans with a funky bandanna holding back his dreads. He would no doubt look more like an arsonist than a property owner to most cops. He was aware of the police car following a short distance behind him.

As he drew closer to the warehouse, his nostrils caught the smell of smoke before he could see any sign of the fire. It appeared to be back lit. After circling around the side, he saw the fire trucks and firefighters first. He looked back at the building. Licks of orange flames crackled and danced, leaping fifteen feet out of the ruins of a large chimney for one of the old kilns. A "womp" sound erupted with a sudden brightness as the fire reached more fuel.

Two firefighters worked at soaking the flames with twin arcs of water. Over the next half hour, bit by bit, the fire died back until it was extinguished. Everyone watching—the firefighters, the police, countless neighbors who'd been awakened by the sirens, and Ash—all stared at the sooty black imprint on the warehouse wall. Ash heard a car door slam and turned to see the State Arson Investigator, Weaver, closing the distance between them.

After a word from the Fire Division Chief, several firefighters cautiously approached the chest-high remains of the chimney. With heavily gloved hands and small rakes, they lifted out clumps of wet leaves and piled them carefully on the ground. After a few minutes, one of them lifted a scrap of rag with his rake and shouted, "I've got something!"

Weaver ambled over and slid on a pair of blue nitrile gloves from his pocket. He held open an evidence bag, collected the scrap, then sniffed it.

Ash watched him carry the bag to his car and return with a flashlight. Weaver squatted down and directed the light onto the mound of wet leaves the scrap had come from. He peered at what looked like a white stick. He lifted one edge in his gloved hand, caught his breath and set it back down. "Stop!" He ordered. "Stop all work." He waved over the two cops who had shown up at Ash's house and said something to them quietly. They looked down at the stick before hurrying back to their squad car.

Ash moved closer to Weaver. "What did you find?" To his surprise Weaver gave him a real answer. "A bone. Looks human."

# Chapter 22

Early the next morning, the abrupt sound of a jazz saxophone coming from her cell phone woke Iris from a deep sleep.

"Uh huh," she mumbled into the phone as she felt Luc roll over toward her. The screen on the phone in the dim light read six thirty-five. *Ugh.*

"It's Ash. Did I wake you?" His voice sounded shaky. "I'm outside your place. Is it OK if I come up? Something's happened."

Iris sat up. "Sure. Give me a minute to get dressed."

Luc mumbled, "Who's that?"

"Ash is here and needs to talk. Go back to sleep."

Instead, Luc lumbered out of bed himself while Iris threw on her jeans and a sweater. She buzzed the front door to unlock it and Ash came in and climbed the staircase.

He was wearing what were clearly his painting clothes and looked as though he hadn't slept all night.

"Are you OK?" Iris asked.

She saw fear in Ash' eyes but he nodded. "I think so."

Luc, now dressed, moved behind them into the kitchen. "I'll make some coffee."

"I'm sorry to bother you guys with this. It's not your problem."

"Let's go sit in the dining room," Iris said. "Tell us what's happened."

Ash sat down, but it took him an eternity to speak. His hands fiddled with the bandana holding back his hair. He finally slid it off and stuffed it in his pocket.

When Luc slid a mug of coffee in front of him along with a carton of milk and a canister of sugar, Ash wrapped his hands around the mug as if he needed the warmth. "There was another fire last night."

"No-o-o," Iris breathed out.

"Not a big one this time. It was in the base of that old chimney near the brick kiln foundations."

*Just where Milo and I were poking around yesterday. And that guy was spying on us.*

"Someone poured a bunch of gasoline down there, tossed in some rags and lit a match. But the firemen put it out in half an hour. The Arson guy, Weaver, showed up."

Luc set two more cups of coffee on the table and took a seat.

"How much damage did it do to the building?" Iris asked.

"The fire was the least of it. When the firemen were emptying leaves to check for burning embers, they found a human bone. After going through more of the leaves, they found a skull and then the rest of a skeleton!"

"Oh my God."

"The face had some dried-out skin left on it, some teeth and this long brown hair." Ash closed his eyes as if to blot out the memory. "It smelled awful. I couldn't tell if it was male or female."

He stared gloomily into his coffee, then knocked it back. "I can't believe there was a dead body on my property! The place is cursed!"

"It is *not* cursed," Iris assured him. "What happened next?"

"After the CSI guys in the white suits found most of the bones, a detective from the Medford police showed up and asked me a bunch of questions. He wanted to know where I was earlier that night. I was home working on a new painting. By myself. Then the detective and Weaver got into a pissing match over who had jurisdiction, Homicide or Arson. That's when I left and walked home." Ash ran his fingers through his hair. "I'm totally freaked. I can't figure out if someone is trying to set me up. Should I get a lawyer?"

"Listen—I didn't get a chance to tell you yet but Milo and I were looking at that chimney yesterday to use for storm water retention and we noticed someone in the woods watching us. He ran away when we tried to approach him."

Luc shot her a concerned look.

Iris continued, "I went to Weaver's office afterward to talk to him about the first fire and I mentioned the suspicious person watching the backyard through binoculars. I even gave him the blurry cellphone photo I took of the guy. So Weaver knows that someone else was paying attention to that chimney while you were busy in classes down at UMass."

Ash let out a deep breath. "Iris, you're like my guardian angel. You don't know…it doesn't take much for the cops to circle around someone like me. I could see all levels of suspicion in that detective's eyes."

"The police can't arrest you for owning the property where a corpse was found," Iris pointed out. "They'll process the remains to figure out who the victim is, if they can. Then they'll need to find out who had a motive to kill him or her. As long as you have no link to the dead person, you should be in the clear."

Luc spoke up. "Still, we'd like to get you a lawyer, Ash. Just to give you some advice on how to handle the police."

"I can call my brother, who's a lawyer, when his office opens to get his take on what you should do…if anything," Iris said. "One thing I can tell you now is that you shouldn't say a word to the police without a lawyer. And you shouldn't have to go through all this without having family around. Don't you want to put in a call to Haiti, to fill your mother in on what's been happening?"

Luc added, "It might make sense for her to fly back early."

Ash nervously rotated the coffee mug in his hands. "She calls me on Sunday afternoons on a satellite phone. I'd like to wait until then unless your brother thinks that something bad might happen right away. I don't want to worry her."

Iris noted the circles under his eyes. "Do you have any classes this morning, or can you go home and get a few hours of sleep?"

Ash checked the time on his phone. "I have chem at ten. I probably should go crash." He looked over at Luc. "Thank you both for dealing with my wig-out."

They all stood up and Iris said, "My brother's name is Sterling. I'll call or text as soon as I talk with him about whether you need to do anything now about dealing with the police."

Luc gave Ash a one-shouldered "guy-hug" and said, "Hang in there. It's gonna be OK."

After Ash was gone, Iris and Luc traded nervous glances.

"I don't like the sound of this," Luc said. "Someone might be trying to frame him. I'd like to hire Sterling to represent him, not just to give him quick advice."

Iris' tired brain snagged on Luc's sudden protectiveness of Ash. "He hasn't been accused of anything. That might just make him look guilty."

"The poor kid has no one to protect him."

Iris couldn't believe it had taken her so long to think of it. Could Ash be Luc's son? Did Luc think Ash was? How had she failed to see that angle?

She puffed out her cheeks and exhaled slowly through pursed lips. "Did you know that Angelique was pregnant when she left?"

Luc frowned and his eyes were fixed on the floor. "No."

# Chapter 23

"He has my father's eyes." Luc stared into the bottom of his mug.

"You can't be sure."

"That's what I told myself. That Angel could've met someone else after me. But it explains, in a screwed-up way, why she might have left." Luc drew a ragged breath. "It was so freaky just now—seeing Ash running his fingers through his hair just like I do when I'm stressed. And those intense eyes. Just like my father's." He looked up quickly. "Don't worry. I'm not going to say anything to Ash before I speak with Angel. But if I have a kid who's lived nineteen years without us knowing about each other—then I am royally pissed!"

Iris put a comforting hand on his shoulder. "Why would Angelique do that?"

"I don't know, but I intend to find out." Luc got to his feet and gathered their empty coffee mugs. "I'm going out for a while. I need to walk." He came over and his lips brushed the top of her head. "I love you."

"I love you, too."

After Iris heard the door close, she made her way to the living room and sank down onto the sofa. Sheba jumped up and pressed her solid, wriggling body as close as possible to Iris' while her mistress massaged the dog's enormous silky ears.

Why had Luc never mentioned Angelique in the two years that they'd known each other? He'd mentioned his ex-wife from his time in Italy, although she didn't seem to haunt him. Was he embarrassed about Angelique leaving him, or was he keeping her memory to himself, not wanting to relegate her to the category of "old girlfriend" or "baggage" and fully move on?

Iris had baggage of her own, but she was happy to part with it, especially the regrettable husband from her short-lived marriage. She had spent too many years alone, or with the wrong people. She'd been unprepared for the real thing. But now she knew that Luc was the love of *her* life. She had just thrown her fate all in with him and now she might end up being nothing more than his ultimate rebound woman. If that. Angelique was a widow now, a free woman, the mother of Luc's child. She was, no doubt, still gorgeous. Sure, Luc had seemed angry with her today. But what if she had some reasonable explanation for why she had to lie low for all those years? Maybe she'd witnessed a mob killing or something. Would Luc forgive her and want them to finally be a family? Would Iris then become ancient history?

The bleeping alarm on Iris' phone reminded her that Sterling's office was now open. She punched in his number, but his assistant answered and said that he would be tied up in court all morning. Nevertheless, a few minutes later, Sterling called her back.

"I'm on a break and can give you three minutes," Sterling said with his usual charm. "Please tell me you're not in jail."

"I'm not in jail."

"Please tell me you don't have another charity case you want me to take on. You've used up all my pro bono time for the year."

"I need your advice for this very nice boyfriend of Raven's, you know, Ellie's daughter." It was an accurate enough description for now. Iris knew that Sterling liked Ellie. Everyone liked Ellie.

"Two minutes left. Talk fast."

She gave him the short version.

"This happened in Medford last night? Who's claiming jurisdiction—the local police or the state cops?"

"I'm not sure."

"OK, I'll have my paralegal look into it. The artist boyfriend is Ashley Burke? And, Iris, if this takes more than an hour someone's going to have to pay for my office's time."

"Understood, Bro'," she groaned.

# Chapter 24

An hour later, Iris finally dragged herself up off the sofa. She headed out to the *Leaf and Bean Emporium* three doors away to buy a box of Milo's favorite green Yogi decaf tea. It was the only thing she'd ever seen him drink in the six months that they'd worked together. Then she sat down and called him.

Now, at ten-thirty, Iris was once again sitting at her dining room table, this time facing Milo as he sipped his tea and considered her words. "Harcon offered to protect the site with his private security goons?"

Iris held her coffee cup at a thoughtful angle. "Which may not even be necessary after what happened last night."

Milo looked at her expectantly.

"It explains why someone was watching us yesterday and might also explain why the first fire was set."

"*First* fire?"

"Remember the old chimney foundation we were looking at yesterday?"

"Uh, huh. My memory stretches back that far, more or less…"

"There was another fire set last night inside that chimney. When the firefighters put it out they discovered a skeleton buried under the dirt and leaves."

"What?" Milo looked taken back. "I put my hand inside that chimney!" He reflexively wiped his hand across his black leather pants. "Oh, that makes this whole situation *so* much better."

"Given the condition of the corpse, it was dumped a while ago. When Ash bought the property and word got around that he was going to fix it up, the killer must have gotten nervous and tried to burn down the whole place to hide the evidence. And when that didn't work, and he saw you and me poking around the chimney yesterday, he must have panicked. So he lit another fire last night but, again, it was put out before it could get very far. The police were able to find and take away what was left of the body."

Milo leaned back in his seat, slowly crossing his long legs and staring at the ceiling.

Iris continued, "So, the cops' removal of the corpse also removes the killer's incentive for sabotaging the site—right?"

"Whoa, whoa, whoa…But they didn't catch the guy last night, right?"

"Doesn't matter. As far as we know, his reason for messing with our site is gone. There's nothing left to hide."

"What makes you think he hasn't left evidence or buried

other bodies on the property? What if he, or she for that matter, is some kind of serial killer?"

Iris thought about that for a moment. "Law of averages. Serial killers are actually quite rare. Besides, I'm sure that the cops will search the property and have cadaver dogs go over the site to make sure it's clear of any other guests."

Milo wagged his finger at Iris, a grin on his face. "Only you can spin the discovery of a dead body on a construction site as a good thing. Look—if you can guarantee that Harcon's security will monitor the site, I guess I'm in."

# Chapter 25

Iris spent the rest of the afternoon running Sheba briskly around Fresh Pond Reservoir—much to the short-legged dog's annoyance and the cause of several sit-down protests—followed by a strenuous brown belt class at the dojo and a long one-on-one sparring session. She arrived back at the apartment thoroughly exhausted and was making herself a cup of tea when her cell phone buzzed.

"Hi, this is Walter. I'm a paralegal in your brother's firm. Mr. Reid asked me to get some information from the police about the human remains found on your client's property last night."

"Any luck?" Iris turned off the stove as the kettle started to whistle.

"The detective in charge, Rafael Gonzalez, is about to go public with a press conference, so he was willing to share what they have so far. They lucked out with an identification. Dental records ID'd the teeth as belonging to a young man named Terrence Jones."

"Hang on." Iris grabbed a pad of paper and pencil from a kitchen drawer and scribbled down the name.

Walter continued, "No one had reported him missing. He was living in Medford Square with a girlfriend, both heavily into drugs. She was off on a drug binge when he disappeared and isn't excited about the idea of interacting with the police."

"Could they tell what killed him and when?" Iris lay one of the green tea bags she'd gotten for Milo inside a teacup and poured in the hot water.

"They found a bullet hole in his back. Someone shot him at close range with a thirty-eight revolver. Bullet went through his heart. It wasn't recent—they're estimating maybe four months ago. The forensics techs should be able to pinpoint the timing better. The police are hoping to get more information from the public after they publicize his name. Mr. Reid suggested that you find out if Ashley Burke knew this Terrence Jones, and to warn him, regardless, not to talk to the police without having an attorney present."

"That means that Jones was killed before Ash owned the property. Does Sterling think that he needs a lawyer right away?"

"That depends on whether he has any connection to the deceased."

After Walter rang off, Iris called Luc to tell him what Sterling's paralegal had said. Luc's response was just what she'd expected. Her next call was to Ash.

Over the line, Iris could hear a car muffler chugging loudly in the background.

"Hi Iris, I'm in the car," Ash said unnecessarily.

"The police ID'd the body left on your property as a guy named Terrence Jones."

"Terry?" There was a long pause. "Wow."

"Was he a friend of yours?"

"No, he was just a guy I went to school with. After I started college, I'd still see him hanging around the neighborhood. Word was he was dealing Apache and Kryptonite."

"Those are drugs?"

"Yeah, Fentanyl and crack Cocaine…really bad news."

"He never dealt drugs to you, did he?"

"Are you kidding? I've never been into heavy stuff like that. I couldn't paint or do decent schoolwork if I were strung out."

"OK, sorry. I'm only asking because, now that the police have ID'd the body, they're going to want to interview you, to see if you had a connection to him or any motive to kill him. Luc and I would like to hire a lawyer to be there when they call you in."

"You don't need to do that. Lawyers are expensive. I'll figure something out. You're already doing enough for me. Hang on. Let me pull the car over so I can focus on this." In a few moments, the sound of the busted muffler cut out abruptly and Ash continued, "Do you really think just having gone to school with Terry could put me in the cops' cross-hairs?"

"He was found on your property so they'll need to eliminate you as a suspect. It's just a precaution, and there's probably nothing to worry about. But I think it's time to fill your mother in on what's been happening."

"Yeah, I did that this morning after talking to you guys. I'm driving to Logan now to pick her up."

# Chapter 26

The rhythm of the restaurant kitchen had been off, and it was Luc's fault. Earlier in the evening, Louise had dropped a plate of swordfish she'd just collected from the pass. Instead of taking the re-do in stride, Luc snapped at the mortified server, and the kitchen had been in the weeds for the rest of the night. He'd been irritable for several days, ever since finding out about Angelique and Ash, and was taking out his frustrations on the staff. The circulating rumor that the James Beard Award judges were supposed to be making a visit soon added to the tension.

Using tweezers, Luc dotted five perfect star anises and a dozen baby beets alongside his signature pork belly entrée, a dish so delicate it melted on the tongue. He grabbed the squeeze bottle and finished the tableau with a zigzag of bright green fennel-garlic sauce before handing the plate to Louise. She didn't meet his eyes. It was Friday night's last entrée order. Tyler, the pastry chef, was still plating desserts, but Luc's sous-chef, Arnold, had already turned off the burners on the hot line and was wiping down the stainless steel counters.

It was eleven and Luc was exhausted, but he still needed to make the rounds of the dining room, chatting with each table to provide them with a personal cap to the evening. He shoved his apron in the locker room hamper and checked out his whites in the full-length mirror.

Arnold popped his head into the small room. "Did front of house spot anyone ordering a single glass of wine tonight?" The James Beard judges were known to keep clear heads during their evaluations.

"I don't know. No one's talking to me. I think I've pissed off the entire staff."

"Go make it up with Louise." Arnold shot him a concerned look. "You OK?"

Luc muttered, "It's just the James Beard stress. Sorry I've been such an asshole. Let's all go over to Temple Bar tonight. I'm buying."

Then he nailed on a smile and headed out into the dining room.

Forty minutes later, Luc sat at the nearby bar, wedged in a large circular booth with seven of the Paradise staff who'd chosen to keep the evening going instead of heading home.

He sipped a glass of Pinot Noir while wondering how long he should stay to appear sociable. He usually enjoyed going out with his team after work, winding down together while talking shop. But, for the moment, his mind was on other things.

One of the younger waitresses, Jess, came back from the ladies' room. She reminded Luc a little of Angel, with her fine features and petite build, although he hadn't made that connection when he'd hired her the previous summer. Jess giggled loudly as she slipped back into her seat and brushed a trace of white powder from her nostrils. Coke—the scourge of the restaurant world. Luc had done his share of partying during his fifteen years working in restaurants, although he'd never used during service. But he was also the son of a vice cop and had heard enough horror stories to keep his indulgence within bounds. These days he only smoked an occasional joint with friends after an Ultimate Frisbee game.

By their senior year, Angel's friends had gotten into the serious stuff. Shania, Juan, Bruno and Maggie would hang out in Juan's basement apartment on weekends experimenting with percocet, oxy, or whatever prescription painkillers Juan's older brother, a nurse, could get his hands on. Angel had been open with Luc about what was going on, but had assured him she was just hanging out, not using. She wouldn't wreck her future going down *that* rabbit hole. Still, she refused to turn her back on the friends she'd had since grade school either. She didn't want them to think she'd gotten stuck up since they'd moved her into Honors classes.

Luc would have wanted to spend as much time as possible with his girlfriend regardless, but he was also eager to keep her away from temptation. She had such big dreams for her life, and he wanted to protect those dreams. Yet Luc's parents made it clear that he needed to spend some of his weekends on family obligations. That meant he'd worry about what Angel was doing as he pushed a lawn mower back-and-forth in neat rows or jiggled his foot impatiently while seated in a church pew.

Twenty years ago, he'd wondered if Angel's disappearance had had anything to do with that troubled crowd of friends. Most of them had scattered after graduation, and Shania was the only one he'd ever been able to track down. She'd been a dead end.

Luc looked up from his wineglass and scanned the faces around the table, young men and women in their twenties, buzzed on service adrenaline and coke, in varying stages of maturity. Ash was not much younger than them. From what he could tell, he was a solid guy—loving, talented and hard-working. Angel had done a good job raising him. But Luc couldn't help believing that, if he really was Ash's father, he would have made their life better and easier if he'd been a part of it.

# Chapter 27

The next morning during breakfast, Iris told Luc that Angelique was back from Haiti. As tempted as he was to toss his half-finished bagel into the compost bin and drive over to her house immediately, he continued chewing and even made a point of drinking another cup of coffee before ambling off to get ready for the day. He regarded his thirty-seven-year-old face in the mirror as he shaved the blond stubble from his cheeks. How would Angel react to seeing him after twenty years?

Luc got into the van and followed its GPS for six miles to the address in Medford. He hadn't called first to announce his arrival and now his hands were sweaty on the steering wheel. Angel would have no warning or get any chance to back out of talking with him.

He stood nervously in front of the small, whimsically painted cottage, and eventually summoned up the courage to walk up and ring the bell. When the door flew open a moment later, Luc stood before Ash who was clearly surprised.

"Uh, Luc? Can I help you?"

"Hi, I actually came to see your mother, if she's here."

"Is this about the lawyer? It was nice of you to offer, but…"

A voice from behind him called out, "Who is it, Ash?"

"It's me, Angel. Luc."

Ash stepped aside to let him in. Angel stood a few feet away, in the doorway to a room beyond. In frayed jeans, bare feet and a *Bonjour Cap Haitien!* T-shirt, she looked tiny and tired. She had aged a bit. Her face looked chiseled now, but to Luc that made her even more beautiful. He wanted to go to her, to wrap his arms around her.

Ash looked back and forth at the two of them, his eyes growing wide, then grabbed his coat from a peg by the door. "I think I'll go out for a while. That OK, Mom?"

"Sure." Angel whispered, not taking her eyes off Luc.

Luc leaned against the door frame through which Ash had just left, not sure how to start. When he spoke, his voice croaked slightly. "Been a while, Angel."

His old nickname for her produced a ghost of a smile. "You found me." She closed the small distance between them and raised her hand as if to rest it on his chest, then pulled it back, as if remembering an unspoken warning. "Let's sit down." She led him into the living room, just off the front door.

They faced each other from either end of a sofa, Angelique sitting cross-legged. Twenty years melted away. He knew this woman. The bond was there.

"You still look like you," she said, wistfully.

"You too." Luc wanted to stay in this suspended state forever, drinking her in, sailing right over the passage of years. Nearly overwhelmed by her proximity, he didn't want to jeopardize the moment by asking tough questions, but he needed answers. Finally, he said, "Did Ash get a chance to fill you in on the trouble at the warehouse?"

Her eyebrows pulled together in concern. "He did. I understand that you and your girlfriend volunteered to hire him a lawyer."

Angel's mention of Iris pulled him out of his reverie. He remembered why he was here. "There've been two fires on the property and now they've found a decomposed body out back. The police have been asking Ash for an alibi."

Her lips pursed. "Yeah, the cops do that when there's a young Black man around to maybe pin a crime on."

"That's why I'm offering my help. But I don't want to butt in if you think that this is none of my business." His eyes were locked on her face. He could see a battle going on inside of her. "You left me twenty years ago. Ash is nineteen. Is he mine?"

Then, as if Angel had made up her mind, one corner of her mouth ticked up. "Always a wiz at math, Cormier. Yeah, you're his father."

Suddenly tears were brimming in Luc's eyes. "My God, Angel. Why did you leave? We could have been a family."

Her eyes welled up too, but she remained on her side of the sofa, arms wrapped tight around her knees.

"I could have handled it,"

"I'm so sorry," she finally stammered. "But we can't go back in time."

"That's no answer." Luc said huskily. "I need to know what happened, why you left."

"I can't explain it to you right now."

He looked at her incredulously. "Right now? I've been waiting twenty years! I missed my son growing up. How can you tell me I have to *wait!*"

She remained silent, looking pained.

"That's bullshit. Why can't you answer me?"

Angel looked away from him. "I'll tell you everything soon. I promise."

# Chapter 28

I ris noticed that when Luc left the apartment that morning, he was wearing the robin's egg blue cashmere sweater she had given him for his birthday—the soft one that made her want to run her hands over his chest. He'd mumbled, "I'll be back soon," and dropped a kiss distractedly on the corner of her mouth before heading down the stairs.

As Iris heard his van chug quietly away, she screamed "I HATE THIS WOMAN!" Sheba looked up with her baleful eyes from a spot at Iris' feet. She got up on her stubby legs and let out a low, all-purpose growl.

"I know. I have to be a grown up." Iris sighed as she explained everything to the dog. "But she left him years ago and she can't just waltz back into our lives and take him back now."

With all that thoroughly clarified for the bewildered Basset hound, she cleaned up the breakfast dishes and glanced at the clock display on the microwave. Only forty minutes until she was scheduled to meet with Alex Harcon's engineer over at Ash's warehouse in Medford. His security team would be there too, setting up their cameras. She'd invited Milo to join them, but he'd said he wasn't sure if he'd be free on this Saturday morning. He'd try to make it. Iris wondered briefly just what his availability depended on.

When she pulled up to the building site, she saw Milo's motorcycle already parked out front but there was no sign of him. She trudged around to the back of the building and found him examining the scorched brick wall behind the half-demolished kiln chimney.

He looked up as she approached. "What's wrong?"

Iris couldn't rid her mind of the thought of Luc and Angelique having an emotional reunion at that moment several blocks away. She could practically feel the vibes coming from the direction of Angelique's cottage. Yet she lied smoothly. "Nothing."

"Iris, there's steam coming out of your ears. Did I do something?"

"No, no, everything's cool with the project. I'm glad you're on board."

Milo cocked his head to one side but said nothing.

"We'd better wait out front for the others," she added.

As they rounded the building, a black Tesla slid silently into the parking space behind Iris' Jeep. Two sleek, black-clad men emerged from the front doors.

She approached the men, hand extended to the one who'd

been driving. "I'm Iris Reid, the architect for the project, and this is Milo Miller, the general contractor."

The driver introduced himself as Fritz something, a Harcon engineer, and the blond brawny passenger was Mike, the Harcon security guy. They both had extra firm handshakes. Mike removed a large suitcase from the trunk, looked over at Milo's bright blue motorcycle and said, "Nice bike. Belong to one of you?"

When Milo admitted ownership the two of them started talking motorcycles as they wandered around the outside of the property, scoping out locations for the surveillance cameras.

Iris unlocked the warehouse's front door and led Fritz inside. When she offered him a set of drawings from her tote bag, he politely waved them aside. "Alex already sent me the PDFs." He peered up at the existing roof with its ragged hole, patched over with plywood, pulled out his phone and started punching different buttons. He pointed the phone at various surfaces, and spoke to it with terse voice commands.

Iris had to ask, "Are you taking measurements with your phone?"

Fritz looked surprised. "You don't know about this iPhone RoomScan app? It's a game-changer." He demonstrated how it worked.

*She needed to update her work tools.*

Across the open space, Mike hoisted the on-site twenty-foot ladder up onto his shoulder and headed out the back door, followed by Milo who was rolling Mike's suitcase behind him.

It took Fritz less than an hour to document every measurement he might need using his fancy phone app. In that time, Mike installed eight separate cameras, most aimed at the perimeter of the property, before rolling the now-empty suitcase back to the Tesla. The efficient Harcon team shook hands with them again and silently glided away.

Milo watched the disappearing car. "They flew all the way out here from California for an hour's worth of work? Not very green if you ask me."

"Specialists." Iris shrugged.

"Want to go get coffee? Ash tells me there's a great vegan place nearby."

Iris figured that was probably a more sensible idea than driving past Angelique's place to see if Luc's van was still there. "Sure, I could use another caffeine infusion."

Iris directed Milo along the now-familiar route to the Healthy Planet café. The Saturday lunch crowd was there in full force and they were lucky to grab a just-vacated table in the back. Milo checked out the Christmas tree lights garlanding the windows and the gaudy red Naugahyde booths. "Not how I picture a vegan restaurant."

Iris laughed. "But the food's good. And they might even have that oddball tea that you like."

She could see Maggie taking orders over on the other side of the room, but a second waitress, much younger, with a mousy brown ponytail, came to wipe down their table and distribute menus. "I'll be back in a minute to take your order."

"Want to get lunch?" Milo asked after looking at the choices. "They have veggie burgers and meatless lasagna. I think I've discovered my work canteen for the next five months."

"Maybe I'll get a cup of vegetable soup." The inescapable thought of Luc meeting with his long-ago lover had made her lose her appetite, but she could probably choke down some soup.

Milo lay down his menu. "So, why were you so upset this morning?"

The previous summer, Iris had learned more than either of them had wanted her to about Milo's girlfriend. Plus, they had bonded over Luc's restaurant renovation. They were friends, sort of. She decided to risk opening up. "Luc's old girlfriend has come back into the picture."

"Oh, shit. You guys are living together."

"It's not like he's left me. She disappeared twenty years ago and Luc just discovered that she lives here in Medford."

"Twenty years? What was he, a kid then?"

"A precocious teenager."

Milo leaned forward. "That's ancient history. First love always feels like the biggest deal when you're young, but then you move on."

Iris decided not to mention that, odds were, they'd had a kid together. And that the kid was Milo's new client. "I know. You're right. I'm sure it's nothing to worry about."

A woman entered the restaurant and looked around

frantically, then spotted Maggie. The woman was an older version of the girl in Luc's photographs—unmistakably Angelique. She gestured toward the kitchen and Maggie nodded her head.

Milo asked, "Who are you staring at?"

"I don't believe it. It's her," Iris said. "The old girlfriend."

Milo turned and checked out the woman striding past their table.

"*That's* her? Hot Damn."

# Chapter 29

When Iris got home after lunch with Milo, Luc was slumped on a stool in the kitchen, a half-empty bottle of wine open in front of him.

Iris hung up her parka. "How'd it go?"

Luc ran his hands over his face.

*So much for the passionate reunion she'd been imagining.*

"Looks like I *am* Ash's father. I got that much out of her."

Iris slipped onto a stool next to him. "Oh, Babe. Did Angelique say why she left?"

"She said she couldn't tell me now."

"Why—is she in the witness protection program or something?"

Misery radiated off of him. "I finally find her and she won't tell me why she disappeared."

They sat locked in glum silence for a long moment.

"How about Ash? Did she tell him about you?" Iris asked.

"I don't know. I was so frustrated, I walked out." Luc took another swallow of wine. "My head feels like it's going to explode."

Iris stood up. "Let me make you some coffee. You just need to get through dinner service tonight. Then you'll have two days off to unwind. When you feel like it we can talk things through."

Iris filled the espresso maker with water and tamped down coffee in the heavy metal filter. "Speaking of Angelique, I was having lunch with Milo at the vegan restaurant near Ash's building and I saw her come in. It must have been after you talked with her."

Luc looked confused. "How do you know what she looks like? Was she with Ash?"

Iris improvised quickly. "I saw a photo of her in Ash's studio the first time I was over there. She seemed upset. She motioned to Maggie to meet her in the kitchen."

"Wait—Maggie Collins?"

"Maggie, the-one-who-owns-the-vegan-restaurant. Apparently they're good friends. Ash says he practically grew up with Maggie, Bruno and their son."

"Fucking A! She left *me* and went off with *those two* twenty years ago?"

# Chapter 30

At nine the next morning, Luc's cell phone rang at an inopportune time. Iris and Luc froze.

"It might be important," Iris said, carefully disentangling herself and sitting up.

Luc groaned and managed to grab the phone from the bedside table. "Uh huh?" he said in an annoyed tone.

She could hear a woman's voice on the other end. Luc sat up in bed and turned his back to Iris. "What time?…I'll call the lawyer and get back to you…No, no, I'm glad you called. Tell him not to say anything."

He turned back to Iris. "A detective from Medford Homicide asked Ash to come down to the station for questioning at one this afternoon. I know it's Sunday, but do you think Sterling could go to Medford to represent him?"

Later that afternoon, when Iris returned from walking Sheba, Luc was standing in the hallway waiting for her. "Any word from Ash or Sterling on how it went?"

"Not yet." But just as she hung up the dog's leash, a jazz ringtone cut through the silence. She dug her cell phone out of her pocket.

It was Ash, but he sounded different, more tentative. "Is it OK if I come over to talk with you guys now? I need to tell you what happened at the police station and there's the whole business about…well, Luc and me."

"Sure, come on over. We'd love to see you."

Twenty minutes later, the doorbell rang. Luc waited at the top landing while Ash climbed up the staircase. When he reached the top, Luc gave him an awkward one-arm hug.

Iris gave Ash a wave from the living room. "Let's sit in here, OK?"

Ash sat in a chair across the room and Sheba chose to nestle at his feet, looking up at him with her doleful eyes. He hunched forward and flashed Luc a quick side-eye. "My mother told me that you're my uh, biological father and about why you weren't around when I was growing up."

"I wish I could've been." Luc looked at Ash's face intently. "I didn't even know that your mother was pregnant with you and then I couldn't find her. She still hasn't told me why she left. But I want you to know that I never would have abandoned you or Angel. And if you'll let me, I'd like to be a part of your life now."

Ash made a slight nod.

"I've heard that you had a great step-father and that he and your mom were your family. But I hope that we can find a way to build up some kind of relationship now."

"I think I'd like that." Ash said thoughtfully. "You guys have been so much help to me these last few weeks, with the renovation, the fires and now with this lawyer." He looked over at Iris. "He's amazing, your brother. He looks like…but then…"

Iris laughed. "I know. Sometimes you need a 'suit' who knows his stuff and knows how to deal with the police."

Ash cracked his knuckles and thought a minute. "Iris, I wasn't completely straight with you. The dead guy, Terry Jones, wasn't just a classmate. He took boxing lessons with Jamal and me in high school. Jamal stopped going after freshman year, so Terry and I ended up being paired a lot as sparring partners during our sophomore year. He dropped out after that and started hanging out with a bunch of assholes, so I kept my distance from him. At the police station, the cops said that they'd heard we used to go rounds in the ring together. Made it sound like there was some kind of rivalry which there definitely wasn't. Then Detective Gonzalez said there'd be more information about the case tonight on the six o'clock news. Mr. Reid wants to meet again tomorrow to go over strategy after seeing what this big announcement is."

The room was silent.

Ash looked from Iris to Luc. "Terry Jones was a rage cage, but I didn't kill him. Still, I'm afraid that the cops are going to find some way to pin this on me."

Luc leaned over and squeezed Ash's shoulder. "We're not going to let that happen."

# Chapter 31

Ellie arrived at the apartment at about five-thirty that afternoon. "Tell me what's going on," she whispered when she'd reached the stair landing. "Where's Luc?"

"Downstairs dealing with restaurant paperwork." Iris hung her coat on the newel post and led Ellie into the living room. "He'll be up before the six o'clock news comes on."

"You didn't say much on the phone." Ellie sank into an armchair while Sheba settled at her feet, her tail rhythmically thumping the floor.

Iris sat across from her on the sofa. "Luc met with Angelique yesterday."

Ellie's jaw dropped open. "When did she get back? Oh my God, did she explain why she'd ghosted him?"

"No, she wouldn't tell him why."

"Oh, for Pete's sake!" Ellie threw up her hands. "The poor guy's waited twenty years and she still won't say? What a bitch!"

"She said she would tell him 'soon'."

"What's that supposed to mean?"

"Beats me. But she did admit that Ash is Luc's son."

There was a small, intricate silence.

Iris eyed her friend. "You don't seem surprised."

"Well… Ash almost certainly has a blue-eyed father. Raven told me that Ash is a Taurus with an Aquarius moon—a very artistic combination, by the way. That means an April or early May birthday. And you'd mentioned that Angelique left at the end of the summer. It's simple math that she must have been pregnant before she blew town. And I saw the pictures of those two together. No way was she cheating on him."

"Why didn't you tell me that?"

"You had a lot to absorb. I figured you needed some time to deal with the old-girlfriend-reappearing scenario before you had to sort through possible paternity implications." Ellie tilted her head. "How's Luc taking it?"

"He's a wreck. He'd already guessed that Ash might be his son, but having it confirmed, that he'd missed his kid's whole childhood, is eating away at him." Iris sighed. "Ash just stopped by and they talked. Luc is trying to start some kind of relationship with him."

"That's good—right?"

"Yes, good. But now we're worried about Ash getting framed for the body found on his property."

"Raven's a wreck about that, too. The dead guy was a drug dealer. She's hoping the police chalk up his death to some argument-turned-deadly with a rival or client."

"Except that they've now learned that Terry, the dead guy, and Ash used to be boxing partners at his step-father's club, and the two weren't on the best of terms."

"Uh, oh," Ellie said. "I hadn't heard that. But Raven said that the guy was shot, not punched to death."

"Excellent point. The police told Ash there's going to be a relevant announcement on the news tonight, so I thought we should all watch it together."

"Ash needs a lawyer."

"Luc hired Sterling to go in to the Medford PD this afternoon with Ash when he was asked questions about the boxing club connection."

"So, what does Sterling say about Ash's chances of getting dragged into this?"

"He wants to hear what the big announcement is tonight. There have already been two fires set near the corpse, so someone has gone to a lot of effort to try to get rid of Terry Jones' body. The big question is why."

Footsteps sounded on the staircase and an exhausted-looking Luc appeared in the living room. "Hey, Ellie." He dropped heavily onto the sofa next to Iris and threw his head back. "I take it Iris has told you everything."

"Of course," Ellie said. "I'm so sorry that you got blind-sided, Sweetie, but Ash is an amazing guy."

"It's true." A vein pulsed in Luc's temple. "I think Angel did a good job of raising him."

Iris checked her watch and picked up three remote controls

from a bowl on the coffee table. "What do I press to turn this thing on? As soon as I figure out one system, Comcast changes things." After several fruitless attempts, she handed them all to Ellie.

"Don't you two ever watch TV?"

"Not if we can help it," Iris responded.

Ellie punched a few buttons and the abstract painting across from the sofa transformed into an active TV screen. She flipped through the channels until the local Boston news affiliate's logo appeared.

The newscasters spent the next ten minutes faux-emoting and turning back and forth to each other, talking about boring or depressing international and national news. Luc was first to notice the chyron scrolling silently across the bottom of the screen: *Body Found in Medford Chimney Now Identified.*

The image of firemen spraying water against the back of Ash's building appeared behind the announcer's well-coifed head. "Police have now identified the body found on Thursday in Medford," the reporter intoned. "Firefighters were called to the scene of a suspicious blaze, the second in a week, in an abandoned Medford brick factory. Here, they discovered charred human remains," she enunciated those three words, "which had been hidden inside an unused chimney. The body has now been positively identified as that of twenty-year-old Terrence Jones, a purported drug dealer. He was the son of former Medford Police lieutenant Lawrence Jones, who was coming up for parole soon after serving a 14-year sentence in

Concord State Prison for his connection to the 2005 robbery of safety deposit boxes at Medford Savings Bank. It was the largest bank robbery in Massachusetts history." The reporter thinned her sorbet-colored lips disapprovingly. "Officials are asking for the public's help with anything that anyone may have seen or heard regarding Terrence Jones last August or September. Please contact the tip line at 617-349-3300. Tips may be anonymous."

A drably dressed weatherman soon replaced her on the screen and launched into a detailed discussion about snow flurries in the Great Lakes region. Ellie stabbed the power button and the image metamorphosed back into a colorful abstract painting.

"So the dead guy's father was a dirty cop?" Iris looked from Ellie to Luc. "How will that change the case? Will it affect Ash?"

Luc frowned. "I'd guess that this would open up the field of suspects. A cop who spent time in jail must have had enemies. Any one of them might have killed his son, for whatever reason. And the newscaster didn't bring up who owned the property where the body was found. So maybe the spotlight is off Ash."

Ellie made a half-hearted smile. "I almost feel sorry for Terry Jones. Even in death, his father's activities get top billing."

Iris slid her laptop across the coffee table and powered it up. "Yeah, a father who pulls off the biggest robbery in the state is a tough act to follow. I don't remember hearing about it, do you?"

"It's not ringing any bells," Ellie said.

Luc confessed, "I was too busy working on my beurre blanc in culinary school back then to pay much attention to the news."

Iris rattled some keys on her computer, sat back and said, "OK, here it is—Medford Savings Bank Robbery."

Ellie and Luc squeezed in next to her so they could see the screen as Iris read out loud:

**"Five men, including three former police officers, were arrested today on charges stemming from the 2005 theft of an estimated $15 million in cash and valuables from more than 700 bank safety deposit boxes."**

"Wait—" Ellie said. "Wasn't there a movie about this with George Clooney?"

"That took place in Vegas, not Medford." Iris continued to read,

**"The robbers entered the basement of the bank over the Labor Day weekend three years ago. Working from an adjacent optician's office, they drilled through a concrete block wall. They then crawled through the opening onto the top of the bank's vault and spent seven hours chipping through 18 inches of concrete and steel reinforcement to get into the safe**

**deposit boxes. They drilled through dozens of locks and made off with an estimated $15 million in cash and property. Three police officers and two civilians were eventually arrested and charged with the crime. Medford Police Lieutenant Lawrence Jones, Sergeant John McCarthy and Sergeant Mitchell Flynn, were all reportedly on duty when the robbery took place."**

"Geez…that takes balls. Police officers robbing a bank while they're on duty." Luc knitted his brows. "But does this have anything to do with Terrence Jones' murder?"

# Chapter 32

Angelique felt distinctly uneasy as she watched the TV news in Maggie's living room. "Remember that robbery?"

Maggie nodded. "Fifteen years ago. Wasn't it mob related?"

Ash stabbed the OFF button on the TV remote and the weatherman's image disappeared. "What do you mean? How was the mob involved?"

"The dirty cops hit those safety deposit boxes," Angelique explained, "because that was where the Romano crime family hid the money from their business."

Maggie cut in, "The mobsters were never going to admit how much cash was in the boxes and the blank passports and jewelry I read about would be pretty much untraceable."

A car alarm wailed in the distance.

Jamal's voice rose from down the hallway. "Mom, Dad's calling for you."

Maggie wedged past Ash, picking up three empty dessert plates as she went. "Coming Bruno…"

Ash took a sip from a can of Coke. "Sound's suicidal to me, stealing from the mob."

"They actually got away with it for several years. If I remember right, there was some kind of double-cross later when one got caught and turned in the others. I don't think they ever found the money."

"I never knew that Terry's father was a cop or that he was in the joint." Ash crushed the empty soda can in his hands. "Doesn't excuse him for being such a dick."

Angelique asked, in what she hoped was a neutral tone, "Did you have any contact with Terry last summer? Is there anything the police can use to connect you two? No matter how far-fetched?"

Ash looked to his left and blinked.

"Ashley?" His mother prodded.

"You should talk to Bruno."

Her son suddenly appeared very vulnerable. "I'm asking *you*. Tell me."

Ash sighed. "Terry was supplying Jamal."

Angelique blanched, glanced down the hallway and whispered, "Did Maggie know?"

"I don't think so. The last time Jamal got out of rehab, Bruno asked me to have a word with Terry."

Angelique pressed her fist against her forehead. "Oh, God. Did you threaten him?"

"No one heard me. I just told him…I told him that if he ever sold to Jamal again, he would be very sorry."

"You said 'very sorry'?"

"Not those exact words."

"Oh, Ash." She gave him the universal look of exasperated maternal worry. "Where did you have this conversation?"

"Terry hangs out—used to hang out—in an alley next to a restaurant in Medford Square. I found him there about four months ago. It was after midnight and no one else was around. I'm sure of that."

"I wouldn't be surprised if Lieutenant Lawrence Jones still had good buddies in the Medford Police Department." She steeled herself to ask the next question. "Was Terry fine when you left him?"

Ash's blue eyes blazed. "Yes!" He got up and quickly retrieved his coat from the front hall closet. "I'm going home. I need to talk with Raven."

Angelique couldn't miss how much Ash looked like his father when Luc had stormed out of their house the day before.

She sat thinking for several minutes. Then, reaching a decision, she headed back to the spare bedroom, now set up as Bruno's hospice. She knocked on the door.

"Come in." Bruno's voice sounded feeble. His hepatitis had reached its final stage.

She poked her head in. "How are you feeling?"

He lay under the covers. His gaunt face and pale lips looked like he had a serious vitamin deficiency. Maggie sat at the foot of the bed, a tray propped in front of her.

Angelique surveyed the untouched food with professional

concern. "You should try to eat. Or at least drink the ginger ale." She turned to Maggie. "Could I have a few words with Bruno?"

Maggie, looking at her hard, stood, turned and closed the door gently behind her.

Angelique moved the dinner tray to a nearby table, but she brought the drinking glass back over to Bruno and put a straw between his lips.

He took several small sips and regarded her balefully. "What's the point? I'm dying."

She gave him a hard stare. "I'll tell you what the point is. You convinced my son to warn off Terry Jones from selling drugs to Jamal instead of doing it yourself. Now someone's dumped Terry's body on Ash's property and the cops are sizing him up for a murder charge. You dragged Ash into this, so you're not allowed to die until you damn well get him out of it."

Bruno's skin looked waxy in the glow of the table lamp. "I get it. I know that I've caused so much damage. But I'm going to make things right. I will."

Angelique took a deep, calming breath, which might have worked wonders if she hadn't still been grinding her teeth. It was one thing to forgive Bruno for what he'd done to her. But she would curse his name forever if his actions caused anything bad to happen to her son. "What's your plan? I want details."

He moved his lips wordlessly until he finally croaked out, "You have my word. The boy is gonna be OK. It's better you don't know the details."

"And what about Luc? He's found me now. I have to tell him something."

He clutched at Angelique's hand. "No! After everything you've sacrificed?"

She felt hot tears rolling down her cheeks. "I owe Luc the truth."

"You can't tell him anything. You don't know who Luc Cormier is these days. Things go sideways, you could still end up in big trouble."

# Chapter 33


*six months before*

Fourteen years earlier, Lawrence Jones entered the Concord State Prison with a target on his back. He hadn't just been a cop. He'd been a lieutenant—and one convicted of a major crime, guaranteeing him the hatred of all the prison fiefdoms: the Brothers, the Aryans and, not least of all, the guards. The first month was the worst. He was lucky to have a cell to himself, but during meals or in the yard, the menacing looks and grunts directed his way shriveled his insides. He kept waiting for the outthrust shiv, the razor blade slice, the trio of visitors entering his cell at night, two to hold him down. But they never came. Getting used to the sounds—the clanging of doors, the single screams that ended abruptly, the scurrying of rats inside the walls—left him constantly on edge. Eventually he figured it out. Frankie Romano had to be playing the long game.

That he was still alive, fourteen years later, was pure irony. The Mob had protected him. They must have put out the word on day one that they wanted him to survive his prison term and they would deal with anyone who interfered with that directive. How much longer Lawrence would stay alive after his release and they got their hands on him was another matter.

Of course, some inmates had a looser interpretation than others of what "leave him alive" meant.

It was funny the things that became important to Lawrence during those years. His wife took off right after he was arrested. She hadn't even bothered to divorce him—good riddance. But his kid, Terry, had been there for his dad. His grandmother brought him to visit every other week. Lawrence's mother, Ruby Jones, had been a brick. She'd stepped in to raise Terry even though she'd lost friends over the disgrace Lawrence had brought on the family. Blood mattered to the Joneses. So she'd raised her grandson until her two-pack-a-day smoking habit turned her lungs into overloaded vacuum cleaner bags and she'd keeled over while watching *Judge Judy*. Terry had just turned eighteen when they'd carried the old woman feet-first out of her house, straight into the back of the hearse. Lawrence had been let out under guard on a three-hour bereavement pass so that he could attend her funeral.

Terry had stayed in the small bungalow by himself from then on, still visiting his father at Concord State Prison twice a month. But while his kid had gone through the usual sullen, resentful teenage years—obvious even in the small doses that Lawrence saw—Terry's life after Ruby's death had spiraled downward. He'd resisted his father's recommendation to attend the local community college and didn't seem to have found any steady employment. That suggested to Lawrence that Terry was dealing. His son's increasingly pasty skin and weight loss further suggested that he was doing more than just sampling the goods. Terry had been a good-looking kid before Ruby died. He used to work out at Tavis Burke's boxing club, and Ruby had made sure that he went out decently dressed, not with pants hanging down on his hips and showing his underwear. But now Terry was falling apart, and he was without a father to help him get his bearings.

# Chapter 34



*two months before*

Something was wrong. Terry hadn't been to see him in four weeks. And the last time his kid *had* come, he'd looked totally wasted. Lawrence paced around his tiny, claustrophobic cell, desperate to get out. His parole hearing was coming up in two months, but it might already be too late. Was Terry lying dead in some alley from a drug overdose? The smack, the rock, the meth, whatever—the devil had gotten hold of Terry and Lawrence was the only one who could come out and yank him back from the abyss.

He wanted to phone Clorise Martin, Terry's girlfriend—or his "trap queen" as Terry referred to her, but he couldn't find a contact number for her on the internet in the prison library. From what he'd heard in the yard, no one really had landlines anymore. Everyone carried around their own private pocket phone. Even guys inside had them squirreled away under their mattresses or hidden inside an electric outlet box in the concrete wall of their cell. He'd figure out how this new kind of phone worked the same way he'd figured out his way around a computer. Google was his new best friend.

Lawrence couldn't even contact Mitch Flynn, his old partner, to check on Terry. Mitch had been paroled over two years ago but was long gone—disappeared, vamoosed, no phone number and untraceable. Mitch hadn't waited around to get the McCarthy treatment from Romano's guys who had fingered McCarthy a short six months after the robbery. They had worked him over slowly and, no doubt painfully until he'd given up the names of the whole team and handed over his share of the take. Under those circumstances, Lawrence couldn't blame McCarthy for ratting them out. And, in the end, Romano had still killed the dumb bastard. Luckily, Lawrence had a confidential informant planted among Romano's guys who had given them a heads-up that their cover was blown. But the Medford cops had their own informant and they were able to pick up the robbery team before Romano got to them. Lawrence and his friends hadn't had time to dig up their stashes, but at least they were still alive and they'd still have a nice chunk of change to fund their after-prison lives. If they could only *stay* alive.

The Safety Deposit heist was supposed to have been a no-brainer. Lawrence's confidential informant had told him that the Romano family stored the proceeds from their various enterprises in basement safety-deposit boxes at that bank, safe from the I.R.S.' prying eyes. Jewels and cash were just sitting there waiting to be scooped up. It wasn't like Frankie Romano had legitimately earned the vast sums in those little underground boxes. And Frankie wouldn't want to draw too much attention to a theft, lest the authorities got interested in the source. Besides, no one would ever suspect that cops themselves had been behind the robbery. But, unluckily, McCarthy's girlfriend was a cousin of one of Romano's guys, and the word leaked out.

Dreaming about a new life with Terry was what had kept Lawrence going all these years in the can. He would pore over atlases and travel books in the prison library, fantasizing about where they would choose to live. They would fly off, minus the skanky girlfriend, to some exotic place like Bolivia. Wasn't Bolivia where Butch Cassidy and the Sundance Kid escaped to after one of their last robberies went bad? But then, their story hadn't ended well.

Lawrence would pay his lawyer well to sneak him away and hide him long enough to collect Terry and the money. Then they would blow town forever.

# Chapter 35

On Monday morning, after Iris headed off to the dojo, Luc rinsed his coffee cup and wandered back to their bedroom. He hoisted a cardboard box doown from a shelf high up in the closet. The weak winter sun coming through the shutters cast slats of light and dark on the hardwood floor. Sitting cross-legged on a throw rug, Luc opened the top flaps of the box. His gaze landed on the envelope of photographs labeled "High School-junior year". He slid out the snapshots and held them by their corners. He hadn't looked at these in at least a decade. He began to sift through the prints, then stopped the moment that he found the one of Angel and him with their arms around each other.

God, they were so young. He studied Angel's expression and knew that he hadn't imagined her love for him. How had Angel done it—becoming a mom at eighteen, putting aside her own plans to take care of a baby? What could have possibly made her disappear from him, especially when their child needed him most?

And who was the boy in that photograph? Luc had been a few years younger than Ash was now. He had been so sure about his feelings then. His love for Angel was never going to fade. They would always be together. Their relationship would never be like his parents'. So confident, so romantic, almost smug. As he remembered how those feelings had been crushed, he understood that he had lost more than just Angel.

During his senior year, Luc's grades had gone to hell. He couldn't focus on academics, and all the weed he smoked to dull the pain of Angel's absence and his father's murder didn't help his concentration. He certainly didn't get the scholarship to Berkeley he'd been hoping for. He only got into Johnson & Wales Culinary School down in Providence through the intervention of his junior year English teacher, one of their alums.

Luc packed the photos back in their envelope and continued to go through the rest of his mementos. Midway down he discovered a small, dingy toy dog with one eye dangling from its socket. *Ruff!* Luc had devotedly dragged this stuffed animal around with him way longer than his father had thought appropriate for a boy. He could still remember the day, when he was about four years old, when the toy had mysteriously disappeared. His father had told him he was a big boy now and didn't need Ruff anymore. His mother had evidently saved it and kept it hidden away. Luc stroked its threadbare fur and wondered what neurosis his father's action had left him with—fear of abandonment? There should really be a handbook for parents on how to avoid inflicting misguided damage on their kids.

Digging down deeper, he spotted the fat packet of letters he'd sent to Angel—all of them returned unread. He felt a rush of embarrassment. He extracted them and, after confirming that the envelopes were still sealed, laid them behind him, out of sight. He moved on to examine sports trophies and school reports, family photos and team jerseys, placing them in piles. Finally, near the bottom, he found what he'd been searching for—a practically-new baseball. It wasn't autographed, but it was a treasure nevertheless.

Luc remembered vividly the June afternoon in 1990. He'd been eight, and his father had taken him to a Red Sox game. The Sox were playing the dreaded Yankees and were ahead 15-to-1. It was top of the eighth and Wade Boggs had stepped up to the plate. Luc was standing on his bleacher-seat so he could see. Wade swung and tipped a foul into the stands directly at them. His father stretched out his bare hand and caught the ball, slapping his palm so hard it throbbed for a week. But he had wanted so badly to get that ball for his son. Luc had given it pride-of-place in his room right up until his father was killed. Then, he'd stuffed it away deep in a drawer to avoid having to look at such a painful reminder.

Luc returned the pile of mementos to the box and the box to its shelf, but carried the baseball and the letters down the hall. He would find a place to display the ball and burn the rest.

Half an hour later, Luc pulled into the narrow driveway of his sister's tidy Dutch Colonial a few blocks from their mother's house. How could Mary have stayed within such a tiny orbit? Wasn't she curious about what else was out there in the world? Still, it was probably good for his nieces to live close to their grandmother. Not having kids had given him more freedom— *then he remembered.*

Mary answered the side door after his first knock. She asked, "You OK?"

"What—I need a reason to visit my favorite sister?"

She rolled her eyes.

Luc followed her in through the chaotic mudroom to the cheerful kitchen with soccer schedules, artwork and class pictures of his two nieces adorning the refrigerator. He dropped into a chair and eyed a familiar-looking coffee cake in the center of the table. He leaned forward and sniffed it. "Grandma Karlsson's recipe?"

"Uh huh. You want coffee?"

"I'm good."

She cut fat slices of cake and slid a plate over to him.

He tasted it. "Not bad."

"Really?"

"A little heavy on the cardamom, but Grandma's always was."

Mary tossed a cloth napkin at him. "How does Iris put up with you?" She sat back in her chair and rotated her index finger in a get-on-with-it-and-tell-me gesture.

Luc crushed some crumbs intently with his fork. "Do you remember Angelique Jackson from school?"

"Your first girlfriend, the one who broke your heart, right?"

"What did Mom and Dad think of her?"

"Why are you asking? You two went out together ages ago."

"Humor me," Luc said with a shrug of his shoulders. "Do you remember anything they said about her? Our parents weren't the world's most open-minded people."

"True." Mary hesitated before speaking. "You brought Angelique over for dinner one time when I was back from college. It might have been the first time they'd met her. After you left to walk her home, Mom said something to Dad about how you should stick to your own kind."

Luc set his mouth in a line. "What did Dad say?"

"That this was just your first girlfriend. It wasn't as if you were going to marry her."

He stared out the window and sighed.

"But then they changed. You guys stayed together and I think they started to like her. Or at least Dad did. He said that Angelique was a good influence on you. Your grades were up and you wanted to go to a good college. That surprised the hell out of me because I'd always thought that Angelique Jackson ran with the druggie crowd. But I certainly never told that to Mom or Dad."

"Angel wasn't into serious drugs. She just had friends in that group."

"Why are you thinking about her all of a sudden?"

"Because I finally discovered where she went."

Mary's head jerked back. "You were still looking for her?"

"No, but I always wondered what became of her."

"So, where was she? What's the story?"

Luc told her what he had discovered.

Mary's eyes widened, and her mouth dropped open.

He gave her a long look.

"I have a nephew? You're a father? Why didn't we know about this?"

"I'd like to know that myself."

"Oh God, Luc. What a shock for you!"

"I'm trying to get to know Ash, but his life just got real complicated. Did you see on the news that the police found the body of a drug dealer in a chimney in Medford?"

"Rings a bell."

"That happened on Ash's property, an old brick factory, and he knew the guy. So now the police keep calling him in for questioning. I hired Iris' brother to act as his lawyer."

"The police suspect Ash of *murder*? Holy crap! Is that why Angelique reappeared—to find you and get your help?"

"It wasn't like that. Ash told Iris that his mother had gone to high school at Rindge & Latin and we figured out who she was. I went to see Angel, and she pretty quickly admitted that I was Ash's father. The timing works out. I think I can even see parts of Dad in his face."

Mary gave him a rueful smile and sighed. "And Iris? This can't be what she signed up for when she moved in with you."

"I know." Luc squeezed his eyes shut. "God, I know."

# Chapter 36

When Lawrence passed through the sallyport for the last time, only his lawyer was there to meet him. He knew that it had been too much to expect, but something solid in his chest buckled a bit. Victor Brus, a slight man with a long beaky nose and close-set eyes, waited while Lawrence collected his personal effects from fourteen years long past and they headed toward the exit stairway. On their way to the underground garage, Lawrence turned to Victor. "Find out anything about my son?"

"Terry sold Ruby's house two years ago. Did he tell you?"

"No." Lawrence frowned. "Where'd he move to?" He said it as if he believed Terry was still alive, though by now he suspected it was bullshit.

"To an apartment in Medford Square." Victor unlocked the car. "I spoke with the girlfriend but she told me that Terry disappeared at the end of August, hasn't turned up since."

"Did she look for him, or report him missing to the cops?"

Victor gave him a long look. "The girl's a junkie. She

figured that Terry had O.D.'d somewhere." He waved toward the back seat. "The minute we leave the guard booth, you'll need to get down on the floor under that blanket until I can get you someplace safe. Romano probably has guys waiting outside the fence."

Lawrence grunted his agreement. He would pay Victor handsomely for the risk he was taking. He could practically hear his heart jack hammering when the sentry checked over their paperwork and IDs. As Victor drove slowly through the gate, Lawrence dropped to the floor.

Victor found him a furnished cottage in Stoneham near the border with Medford. As Lawrence had instructed, the lawyer had provided staples in the refrigerator, linens on the bed, a laptop, a burner phone, and a pile of nondescript clothes set out on the living room sofa. Last but not least, Victor had left a beater car in the driveway with a collapsible shovel in the trunk and enough gas to get him to the Fells, a nearby 2,200 acre watershed reservation that straddled five towns and had a network of walking trails. Assuming Lawrence could still find the burial spot, he'd soon be able to pay his lawyer back for all of this.

As soon as Victor's car pulled away, Lawrence went to the kitchen to make himself some coffee. As the pot began to percolate, he picked up the phone from the counter and punched in the numbers he'd committed to memory.

Sean Flynn, Mitch's younger brother, was the Desk Sergeant at Medford Police Headquarters. Sean and Lawrence had grown up together, starting back in the days when they would get in trouble with the nuns at Cheverus Catholic Elementary to their teenaged years passing footballs back-and-forth while running around the Malden Catholic playing fields. Lawrence had even saved Sean's life once when a domestic disturbance call had gone sideways and the coked-up husband had tried to stab Sean with a hunting knife. Lawrence had taken the guy down and gotten a gash on the arm in the process. Sean would have been a first pick for their robbery team if he hadn't been out on sick leave with an ankle injury.

It was a good twenty minutes before Sean was able to call Lawrence back from the privacy of his own car in the police parking lot. After the preliminary how-ya-doin' small talk, Lawrence got around to asking what he most wanted to know. There was a long pause on the phone line.

"Look, Larry, I've got some bad news. We uncovered a body yesterday that'd been stashed in back of a warehouse several months ago. The dentals ID'd him as Terry. I'm so sorry, man. He'd been shot in the head with a .38 caliber."

"Oh, shit." Lawrence moaned. "Goddamn Frankie Romano!"

"Yeah, that was our first thought too, given the, uh, situation. But we're thinking now that it wasn't him. I said it was a .38 and Romano's guys generally use .22s. And afterward, there were these lame attempts to burn the body to get rid of evidence. Strictly amateur hour."

"How 'bout the forensics? Did they find the gun?"

"We don't know where Terry was actually hit since the warehouse looks like it was a drop site. No gun was found, and the decomposition's pretty advanced. The fires burned up any other potential evidence. But if it'd been Romano, you can bet we never would have found the body."

"So who are the cops liking for it, Sean?"

"You remember Tavis Burke's son, Ashley? The kid who won all the Junior boxing competitions? There's some evidence pointing his way, but it's not for sure. Might have been about drugs."

# Chapter 37

As Iris jogged along Mass Ave on her way back from the dojo, still revved up from her sparring session, her cell phone played the ominous opening chords from Mozart's Don Giovanni.

"Hi, Sterling," she answered. "Is the mob connection story going to take the heat off Ash?"

"Not so fast, Iris Penelope Winthrop Reid. As your older brother, the only other surviving member of the Reid family…"

She ducked into the nearby lobby of the Porter Square Hotel and made a bee-line for their coffee shop. This was obviously a conversation that would require caffeine and sitting down.

Sterling continued…"I would like to discuss this man you're living with."

"Luc."

"Were you aware before you decided to shack up with him that he had an illegitimate child?"

"Double espresso with room for milk," Iris mouthed to the

barista, the phone wedged between her shoulder and ear. "No, I didn't know that, and neither did he. We're both trying to cope with this news and he's stepping up to the responsibility plate by hiring you to defend his son."

"So this was a youthful indiscretion? It doesn't speak well of his moral character. Didn't he know about taking responsible measures?"

Iris pulled the phone away from her ear and held it up to her mouth. "CONDOMS CAN BREAK!" The heavily tatted young woman handing her her coffee gave her some sympathetic side-eye.

There was a brief pause. "I just hope that you haven't tangled your finances with his after selling our family home. You never asked me to draw up any pre-shacking-up legal agreement. And he is in a highly speculative business, owning a restaurant."

Iris sank into an uncomfortable molded-fiberglass chair and took a deep sip of her coffee. "I'm a grown woman, Sterling. I'll be fine. Now can we talk about the case?"

"No."

"Excuse me?"

"I can't discuss anything covered by attorney-client privilege."

"I'm just asking for your take on last night's TV announcement about Terrence Jones' father. That's information in the public realm, not provided by your client."

"Well…I could say, hypothetically, when a person steals

from nefarious people, it increases the odds of a close family member coming to a bad end. And that, in turn, decreases the odds of that bad end having been caused by a person with a lesser grievance."

Forty-five years of conversations like this flashed through Iris' mind.

"However…" Sterling added.

"However?"

"Terrence Jones' father was released from prison today. If he learns that his son's murder was not a much-delayed meting out of punishment directed at him, then he'll be looking elsewhere for someone to blame."

"Meaning that the father might be even more of a threat to Ash than the police."

"Let's just hope that no stronger motive surfaces connecting Ash to the deceased."

# Chapter 38

Ash parked in the driveway of his mother's house and walked the four blocks to the Healthy Planet. He should probably save his money and eat at home, but he liked patronizing Maggie's place. She needed all the income she could get now that Bruno was no longer driving a school bus. Plus, the food was better than Ash could make for himself, certainly better than the UMass cafeteria. He enjoyed Mondays, coming home after his morning classes to spend the afternoon losing himself in his painting. But he wished he were in his own crib now instead of having to wait until the summer. Living at home was getting old. His mother had been on his case about that fucking jerk, Terry. That guy could make trouble even from the grave.

The restaurant wasn't crowded, and he spotted Maggie pouring coffee at a four-top near the kitchen. She gave him a quick smile and pointed to his favorite booth.

As he slid in, he felt the light bump of someone sliding in after him. He looked over. Shit.

"Hey, Ash. I've been looking for you."

"That right, Clorise? You found me. What's up?" Clearly, by the look of her skeletal body and blotchy face, meth was on the menu. She seemed to have aged a decade since their high school graduation.

"I have a bone to pick with you, Ashley Burke."

Oh, God. He looked around for Maggie. She was taking someone's order on the other side of the room.

"I'm a woman without a man right now and I believe you have something to do with that."

Paranoia—the default state for meth heads, he thought. "What do you think I've done?"

"The cops came to talk to me over the weekend. Told me that my man Terry'd been shot and that it happened several months ago. They found his body by the old brick warehouse. I heard that you'd bought that place."

"And you hadn't noticed him missing?"

Her hardened face turned harder still. "Don't be a smartass. I'm doing you a favor coming here. I figured he'd OD'ed, not got himself shot."

"I'm listening."

"That made me think. Terry wasn't in the safest business, but he knew how to keep his head down, stick to his own territory. Funny thing, though. The night before he disappeared, Terry had a beaut of a shiner. He told me you and him got into it over his dealings with Jamal, said you'd break every bone in his body if he didn't stay away from Jamal."

"And you told this to the cops?"

She smiled, displaying a missing incisor. "I thought I'd come to you first, give you a chance to make it up to me."

"You honestly think I killed him? There must be dozens of people who wanted him out of the way. And why would I leave his body on my own property?"

She lifted a bony shoulder. "Maybe figured you'd be sure that no one found him there. Like I said, I haven't told the cops. Yet."

"So, you're here to shake me down?" He gestured toward the paint-splattered sweatshirt showing through an open coat with frayed cuffs. "Do I look like I have money?"

The wiliness in her eyes was replaced by confusion. Then she ran her hand along his thigh. "Or we could party instead. Make it up to me that way."

He removed her hand and stifled a shudder. Thinking fast, he blurted out, "I'm gay."

"That's not what I heard from the girls at school." She slid her hand under his coat to his crotch and stroked the material on his jeans. No response.

"Maybe you *are* gay."

Ash's eyes were saucers. He choked out, "I came out after I got to college."

Clorise pulled away from him and stood. "You want to play it that way? Fine. Just remember, I gave you a chance first." She stalked out right before Maggie appeared at the booth.

Maggie's gaze followed Clorise out the door. "What was that all about?"

# Chapter 39

The John W. Riggs Municipal rink, at the East edge of the Middlesex Fells Reservation, was empty at this time of night. The memory of Ruby driving Lawrence here for years of early morning hockey practice brought back the smell of her Marlboro Golds, and a wave of sadness washed over him. No mother, no son. A security chain had been strung across the entrance to the parking lot, but it wasn't padlocked. Lawrence was able to unhook it easily, then refasten it behind him.

Along the back edge of the lot, he found the unpaved fire road that led to Wright's Pond. As teenagers, he and his buddies used to climb up this path toward a rocky outcropping to drink beer and smoke whatever anyone had brought along. He'd even brought girls up here to fool around, but never when it was this cold. You could see the twinkling lights of the Boston skyline in the distance.

When Lawrence arrived at the end of the dirt road, he parked the car and lifted an almost-empty backpack onto his shoulder. He glanced back to make sure he was alone. A sliver of moonlight provided enough illumination for his scramble over the rocky surface. When he made it to a tall stone shaped like a giant arrowhead, he reached into his pocket for a compass and switched on his flashlight. He started counting steps as he consulted the compass, moving methodically toward the far side of the clearing in the direction of a dense barrier of evergreens. He managed to squeeze between the closely spaced trees and to keep track of his steps as he navigated down a steep slope. After five minutes of careful movement, he found the place he was looking for and dropped his backpack. He pulled out the collapsible shovel and snapped it into its rigid, extended form.

Lawrence had always been strong and fit, but during his past fifteen years in prison, it had paid to keep himself hard. Still, it was quite a workout to dig a four foot by four foot pit three feet down into the firm dirt. He tested at several sections of the hole by driving the shovel straight down. When he finally heard the dull knock of it hitting metal, he stood, straightened up and stretched out his back. Not quite so young as he once was.

More slowly now, he excavated around the sides of the long-buried ammunition canister, the size of a large briefcase, until he could wedge the tip of the shovel under one end to tip it up. He bent down to tie a rope around it and climbed out of the hole to wrap the other end around a tree trunk. He dragged the heavy steel case up the side of the pit until it sat on the surface, then stared at it. *Had he forfeited all that time he could have spent with his only boy for the sake of this damn box?*

Lawrence's hand cradled the dirt-encrusted combination lock which looped through the case's latch. He'd been keeping six numbers in his head for fourteen years and carefully rotated the cylinders to each one until the lock fell loose. The heavy lid opened as smoothly as the day Lawrence had bought it at a gun shop. Bundles of bills, mainly hundreds, filled the interior, except at one corner where an assortment of jewelry cases and passports from several countries had been wedged in. He stuffed several bundles of the cash into the inside pocket of his parka. Here was his future.

He spent the next twenty minutes refilling the hole and covering it with leaves. After closing the lid of the canister, he wedged it into the extra-large REI backpack and tightened its heavy lower belt around his waist. He adjusted the padded straps as best he could, but much of the weight still pressed down on his shoulders. He worked up a second sweat climbing back up the hill; pausing to rest in the clearing, he started to feel chilled. By the time he backtracked to the car, he was breathing heavily. That's when he saw the headlights aimed at his rear windshield.

He slipped behind a tree and poked his head out. Shit. It looked like a security guard, or maybe a park ranger. In any case, some guy in a uniform was holding a flashlight, looking into the front seat of his car. Had he locked it? The man tried the door, but couldn't open it. He spoke into a walkie-talkie. Lawrence heard a scratchy "old clunker…abandoned."

He pulled off his pack and quietly sat on it, waiting. Was the man going to stay there, killing time until a tow truck arrived? How could he walk two miles unnoticed back to the house with this heavy pack, and what about when they inevitably ran the plate?

He ducked back behind his tree just as the guard/ranger swept his flashlight around in a wide arc. Then the man walked in his direction and stopped. Lawrence heard him unzipping his fly, then peeing loudly against an adjacent tree not six feet away. Lawrence held his breath.

He didn't exhale until the man turned and walked back to his car. The guard started the engine, did a sweeping three-point turn, and drove back toward the skating rink parking lot.

Lawrence remained motionless behind the tree. Only when he saw the taillights disappear around a corner in the distance did he run to his car and take off. At a fork in the road, he turned away from the rink and headed for the secondary exit.

# Chapter 40

Lawrence woke up late the next morning to sunlight pouring in through a window. He was definitely not in a prison cell anymore. He got up and moved his stiff limbs slowly, rolling his sore shoulders back and forth. It was when he was filling the percolator with coffee that he remembered what he'd left inside the trunk of his car the night before. It seemed as good a place as any to leave that steel box for now, but it wouldn't be safe for long. Romano's men were no doubt searching for him at this very minute. Lawrence Jones needed to plan his great escape from the Commonwealth of Massachusetts. But first, he needed to avenge the murder of his son.

His lawyer had given him the address of Terry's last-known apartment. Lawrence wondered if Clorise was still living there. He could hardly drive there, at least not until he'd had a chance to change the license plates on his car. And stealing a set of new plates would have to wait until well after dark. He had been too tired the previous evening to do anything more than pull the car into the garage and fall into bed.

He'd spent the previous afternoon learning how to work all the features on his new cell phone. Really, a handy little device. He used it now to look up bus routes, figuring out the closest route to Medford Center.

How much of a disguise would he need to make sure that none of Frankie Romano's guys spotted him? He'd traded his paunch for some wrinkles and his hair had turned gray. But maybe he'd better shave off his grizzly beard in case someone from the joint had sent Frankie an updated photo of him.

It was late afternoon by the time a clean-shaven man wearing sunglasses and a wool cap stepped off the bus in Medford Center. Lawrence knew that Linden Place was nothing more than a dark alley between rows of cheap apartment buildings. He covered the two blocks from the bus stop and stood in a dingy vestibule that smelled of cat piss, facing a row of mailboxes and buzzers. The name *Martin* appeared next to #2R, but the accompanying *Jones* had been crudely crossed out and replaced by *Maddox*. Looked like Clorise had a new roommate.

Lawrence's thumb on the intercom got no response, so he pushed several random buttons until an annoyed tenant buzzed him in. He knocked on Clorise's door and waited. The pin-hole of light in the fisheye went black. A chain slid. The deadbolt clicked. The door opened a crack to reveal a distrustful, bloodshot eye.

"Clorise? I'm Terry's father."

The eye got big. "You're out of jail?" She opened the door wider to reveal herself, a hard-wrung woman in a pink tracksuit. "Didn't you hear? About Terry?"

Lawrence noticed that she was missing a tooth. Had his son really been living with this woman? "Can I come in?"

Clorise gave him a once-over, then stood aside to let him enter.

The apartment was a shock. A massive oak dining table with six matching chairs filled the front section of the room. In the rear, a sofa covered with a familiar-looking gold flowered fabric had been shoved against the back wall facing a TV. Lawrence felt a physical ache in his chest. Ruby's furniture.

Clorise followed his gaze. "Terry gave me this stuff. You want it back?"

Lawrence stared at three of Ruby's prized porcelain Corgis set in the middle of the dining table like a centerpiece. Spoons, lighters, burners and syringes were arrayed around the dogs. It pained him to see his mother's special things in this wretched setting, but he had no use for them. "Keep it."

The room smelled bad, a combination of weed, rotted food and deferred baths. Paper shades on the two windows filtered out much of the light.

Clorise sat down in one of dining chairs and Lawrence followed suit.

"Tell me everything about how Terry died."

Her eyes looked wary. "I told it all to the cops."

Lawrence leaned forward, his hands clasped between his knees as if he were confiding a secret. "My kid was murdered."

Clorise gulped visibly. Her eyes darted toward a door, probably to a bedroom. Was the *Maddox* person from the mailbox hiding in there?

"I need to find out who did this to Terry." He kept his voice level. "I'm sure you want that too."

She shifted in her chair. "It was last August. One night, he just didn't come home. I'll be honest, I wasn't in such good shape back then."

*Like she's in such good shape now?*

"I didn't know what to do." She tried to make her eyes look innocent, but the effect was unconvincing.

"I'm aware that Terry was dealing, Clorise. Was he worried about anyone coming after him? Was he poaching on someone else's turf?"

"No, no, he wasn't stupid. But there *was* something that happened. I didn't remember it right away, but it came back to me later. Terry showed up the night before he disappeared with a shiner, a big one on his left eye. I asked him about it and he said that Ash Burke had given him a beating and warned him not to deal anymore to his friend, Jamal. I said whatthefuck, Terry. You've got plenty of business. Cut Jamal off." Clorise looked self-righteous. "I warned him."

"Is that true?" He held her eyes. "Do you think Ashley Burke was the one who killed Terry?"

Clorise stared down at the floor and nodded her head. "I'm telling you dead-ass. This went down right before Terry disappeared. Ash was the only one Terry was afraid of."

# Chapter 41

Mid-afternoon, Iris was on-line in her home office searching for a ceramic pendant light fixture to use in the studio kitchens. It was one of the few remaining items left on her shopping list. She found a perfect choice but now would need to convince the manufacturer to donate a dozen of them. Her cell phone's loud beep interrupted her thoughts, signaling a text alert: *Medford site perimeter has been breached. Law enforcement has been contacted.* The sender ID read: Harcon security system.

Oh, hell. What now? She sifted through a dozen business cards in a leather box on her desk before she found it: Mike Maxwell, Associate Director of Harcon Security. She punched in his phone number.

Mike answered as if he'd been expecting her call. "We have a situation at the Burke warehouse. Two trespassers were spotted behind the building near the chimney. One was taking photographs. We'd posted *no trespassing* signs and linked in our cameras to the local cops, so the Medford police sent over a patrol car. They're holding the two men at the property. They'll book the guys if we want to press charges. What do you think we should do?"

"Me? Why is this my decision?"

"We tried to reach the owner, Mr. Burke, but he's not answering his phone. The cops are ready to take the intruders down to the station. Mr. Harcon listed you as the secondary contact person."

"I suppose I could drive over and check out their story," Iris said. "Could you convince the cops to wait a little longer?"

"I'll try. It will save them a lot of paperwork if the trespassers turn out to be harmless. On the other hand, we should make it clear that we mean business about keeping people off the site."

"Did the two guys explain what they were doing there?"

"Not that I've heard."

"Let me see who they are and whether they seem like a threat. I'll call you back."

On her short drive over to Medford, Iris began to worry. What if these men were associates of Lawrence Jones, the dead drug dealer's father—or worse, the crime family from whom he'd stolen? Did she really want to find herself on their radar? She should let Mike Maxwell handle this. Why was she even on the security notification list? This was definitely not part of her job description.

But when she pulled up to the warehouse, she recognized the two sorry souls shivering by the police car. They were none other than the *Globe*'s star reporter, Robert "Budge" Buchanan, and his trusty cameraman sidekick, Shane. She had known Budge from her Dartmouth days and they'd had dealings, not always amicable, over the last few years.

She introduced herself to the fresh-faced officers, one of whom was yawning into his fist.

Budge's face lit up as he recognized her. "Iris, would you please tell Officers Sullivan and Lutz that you know us, that this is just a misunderstanding."

Shane had the grace to look sheepish. "Hey, Iris. Sorry about that picture last spring."

Iris folded her arms across her chest. "I don't recall inviting you to trespass on my client's land, Budge. What are you doing here? I can't imagine that a story about a deceased drug dealer is worthy of your fine reportorial talents."

"Oh, but it's gotten so much more interesting than that. Didn't you know that your young client has just been arrested?"

"What are you talking about?"

Budge leaned back against the cruiser. "My sources tell me that the police have it on good authority that Ash Burke threatened the dead guy right before he went missing."

The officer with the mirrored sunglasses, the one who seemed to be in charge said, "If you recognize these guys, we're going to take off."

Iris held up a finger. "Can I make a quick phone call?"

"Five minutes, Miss. Then we're out of here," Sunglasses

responded.

She retreated to her Jeep and phoned Sterling. He didn't pick up. She called his office and his assistant reported that he was at an emergency meeting with a client.

"At the Medford Police station?"

"I believe so."

After a quick call to Mike Maxwell to assure him that the trespassers were just nosy reporters that she would get rid of, she returned to the group of men.

"It's OK, officers. We're not going to press charges this time. But if they ever trip the alarm again, you can lock them up with my blessing."

She turned to leave, but Budge grabbed her elbow.

"Hang on. Let's go get a coffee or something. Don't you want to have some control over this story? You know, I'm going to write it with or without your input."

Iris faced Budge. "I still don't understand why you're so interested in a small-time drug dealer's murder in Medford. This is hardly front page material. Not even front page of the Metro section. More like the police blotter. Have you sunk that low?"

"Are you kidding? The dead guy's dirty cop father just got sprung from prison and the Romano family is still trying to track down where he hid their money. The son's murder is the perfect excuse to squeeze more juice out of the biggest bank robbery in Massachusetts history. The sparks are starting to fly. And then there's the side story about the young painter scraping together enough pennies to buy this old brick factory, then getting you to turn it into a high-profile charity renovation. I'm telling you, this story is ticking off all the boxes." Budge's eyes narrowed a fraction. "Plus, there's the angle about how *you* tie in with this young painter. Medford isn't exactly your turf. Yeah, I'll bet there's some juice there too."

Iris turned away before Budge could see her reaction. She gave him a backward wave as she got into her Jeep.

# Chapter 42

Iris followed her GPS to the Medford Police station, winding along the Mystic River for two slow miles. She slotted her car into a visitor spot and entered the low beige-brick building. A ruddy-faced man with a horseshoe of red hair sat at the lobby desk behind a template identifying him as Sergeant Flynn.

"Hi. I'm looking for Attorney Sterling Reid," Iris said. "He's representing Ashley Burke. Do you know where I might find him?"

Sergeant Flynn raised an eyebrow and gestured toward a row of utilitarian chairs in the hallway. "Please take a seat while I check on that."

Iris looked over at a figure sitting at the far end of the row. It was Angelique, still wearing scrubs and sneakers under a black down coat. The woman stared at Iris with an uncertain expression. Iris approached with her warmest smile, arm extended. "Hi, I'm Iris. Are you Angelique?"

Her smile was guarded, but she shook Iris' hand. "Thank you for everything you and Luc are doing for Ash. I don't know what we would have done today without your brother's help."

The woman's voice was surprisingly steely. Iris took the seat next to her. "Have you heard any news?"

"The desk sergeant told me that Ash and Mr. Reid are upstairs in an interview room. I left work as soon as my son called. They've been up there awhile."

Up close, Iris could read the tension in Angelique's face, the set of her jaw, the obvious fear in her eyes. It had to be terrifying to have any loved one, much less your Black son, being questioned in a police station about a murder.

The hallway was painted a depressing cinder-block gray. As Iris sat there, staring at the wall ahead, she could hear the distant chatter of voices behind a row of doors. Two uniformed officers emerged from one of them, talking as they strolled past the women, the louder cop tossing car keys to the quieter cop as they headed out the front entry. Iris wondered who had leaked the information to Budge that Ash had been picked up. Maybe the *Globe* had underlings listening to police scanners. Or maybe one of these cops got a "retainer" for passing along possible story leads.

Iris felt very aware of Angelique's presence so close to her, their coats touching. She tried to shake the thought that they had both slept with Luc and wondered if Angelique was thinking the same thing. Surely she was too busy worrying about her son. How much danger was Ash in? What had Budge said—the police had it on good authority that Ash had threatened Terry Jones right before he went missing? Why would he threaten a drug dealer? He'd told Iris that he didn't take drugs. Was he lying? And who was the "good authority"?

Iris turned her head and asked in a low voice. "Did Ash tell you about any threat he might have made to Terry Jones?"

Angelique's eyes got big. "Is that why they pulled him in? Where did you hear about that?"

"From a reporter who was caught taking photos of Ash's warehouse. It must have been leaked from the police. I'm afraid it might be in tomorrow's *Globe*."

Angelique let out a strangled "No!" She bent forward, placing her palms on her forehead.

Iris patted her shoulder. "Sterling will get this straightened out."

The other woman sucked at the air and nodded.

Ten minutes later, Sergeant Flynn padded slowly down the vinyl-tiled corridor toward the women. "Attorney Reid and Ashley Burke will be down shortly."

Angelique and Iris exchanged relieved looks. Sterling must have done some fancy footwork to get Ash released.

Several silent minutes stretched out before they heard the gears of the elevator moving, followed by a clunk as the doors opened. A stony-faced Ash and a grim Sterling stepped out. A plainclothes detective pointed them toward the entry door, then retreated back into the elevator before the doors closed.

Ash headed straight for his mother. "Let's get out of here." He registered Iris belatedly and said, "I'd be in a holding cell if it weren't for your brother." He shook Sterling's hand,

"Thanks, again."

The lawyer nodded. "We'll talk tomorrow."

Iris and Sterling threaded their way to his car. They waited until Ash and Angelique had driven away before speaking.

"How bad is it?" Iris asked.

"The prosecutor wanted to charge him. I'm not sure I completely discredited Jones' girlfriend's testimony. The police think they've added motive to opportunity. Now they're searching for means."

# Chapter 43

Fourteen years inside, planning every step of his escape from Romano, and now Lawrence wanted to chuck it all to go after the Burke kid. He stared out the cottage window at the desolate gray twilight and listened to the wind rustling through dead leaves. He should've been in Bolivia by now.

But seeing Ruby's furniture in Terry's old apartment had affected Lawrence. He wanted to believe that his son had kept those pieces for sentimental reasons, to remember Ruby in all her smoke-saturated glory. Lawrence wanted to believe his kid had a heart. OK, he was a drug dealer, but that was on Lawrence. He hadn't been there to offer fatherly guidance. Maybe he should have funneled Terry some money to live on. During his bimonthly visits, Terry had implied that he was still living in Ruby's house and had found some sort of job, although he'd been sketchy about what kind. Lawrence should have paid more attention to his son's life. Now, instead, he would pay attention to his death.

As the streetlights came on, he watched Sean's car pull into the driveway. Sean sat there with the engine idling as if debating whether to come inside. Lawrence met his old friend at the side door and handed him a can of Sam Adams as they walked into the knotty-pine-paneled living room.

Lawrence cleared newspapers from the sofa. "Sit. You want a glass for that? I got uncivilized in the big house."

Sean shook his head, cracked the beer open and took a sip.

Lawrence told him about his discussion with Clorise and how he was convinced that Ash Burke was behind Terry's murder.

Sean studied the logo on his beer can. "Let the justice system take its course this time, Larry. Gonzalez is so close to getting a search warrant. He'll find the gun at Burke's warehouse or the mother's house and then we'll have more than just circumstantial evidence."

Sean, as always, liked to follow rules. His lack of initiative had held him back in his career, keeping him in uniform instead of rising to detective rank. But Lawrence had always known how to lead him astray. He just needed to convince Sean of the "fairness" of this new mission.

"Gonzalez won't find that gun. Do you really think Burke is stupid enough to keep it around? I've done some checking on him. This is a kid who's bought himself real estate before he's even out of college. And he has a big-deal lawyer. The type who can get the guiltiest of slime balls off with a slap on the wrist. The type who demands a huge retainer up front. Where did that money come from? His hard-working mother, the nurse?

This kid must be working his own side angles."

"Larry, look. You were the smartest detective in our Precinct. You saved my ass during that domestic, so I know I owe you. But I'm not real comfortable with helping you go after this kid."

"It's because I was a smart detective that I trust my gut. He's the doer."

Sean shifted and took a quick swig of beer. "We've never had any trouble from Ash Burke before."

"Because he's too smart. He stays below the radar."

"You think?"

"I believe Clorise's story about Burke beating up Terry before he went missing. What would she gain from pointing a finger at him?"

"Yeah, Gonzalez seemed to buy it too."

"But do you think she'd make a reliable witness? No one's going to listen to a junkie. And what jury will care about convicting someone for killing a drug dealer? They'll probably want to pin a medal on Burke. There's what's legal and there's what's right. The Burke kid needs to pay."

Half-way through their second six-pack, Sean had agreed to drive Lawrence's car while Lawrence himself would do the shooting.

Early the next morning, Sean and Lawrence drove cautiously around the neighborhood several times searching for any sign of Romano's guys or the Medford PD. They parked across the street from Burke's mother's house. Sean had brought coffee and a half-dozen crullers from Dunkin'. Lawrence sat in the back seat blowing on his coffee to cool it off, watching the house, waiting for the kid to emerge.

Around eight, the front door opened. Ash stepped out, looking down as he reached into his pocket. This was the first time Lawrence had seen him in person. He was a tall, broad-shouldered young man. Lawrence had no trouble imagining him beating up his broken-down son. The cop and the former-cop lowered their ski masks into position. Sean eased the old Camry out onto the road. Lawrence hunched down and rested the Smith & Wesson revolver on the open window frame. As Sean cruised slowly past, Lawrence sighted his prey and pulled the trigger.

# Chapter 44

Wednesday morning, Iris and Luc divided up the *Globe*, each of them searching for Budge's article.

"Found it," Luc announced, smoothing out the Metro section.

Iris felt a flash of satisfaction that it hadn't made the front page. She read over Luc's shoulder. A photo showed a middle-aged man in a dark suit and handcuffs with guards at either side. He was glaring down into an open grave.

"That must be Terry Jones' father." Iris skimmed the story. "It says the photo was taken at his mother's funeral several years ago. Budge fills in the bank robbery story and how the police discovered Terry's body last week."

"Do you see anything about Ash?" Luc asked as Iris speed-read the story.

"Oh, damn—here's something." Iris pointed to the fifth paragraph. "Terrence's girlfriend, Clorise Martin, claimed that Ashley Burke, the owner of the property where the body was found, had threatened Terrence the day before his disappearance. They were allegedly involved in a dispute about drugs. The police brought Mr. Burke in for questioning late yesterday, then released him. His Attorney said that Mr. Burke had nothing to do with Terrence Jones' murder. 'Someone hid the body on an empty lot that Mr. Burke later purchased. Clorise Martin, a drug addict known to law enforcement, tried to extort money from Mr. Burke before going to the police with her fabricated story about a dispute.'"

"What a shit that Budge is!" Luc exploded. "He'll get Ash killed. What can we do?"

"I'll call Sterling. I spoke with him last night before he gave Budge a statement. By now, he'll have seen this article."

Iris got no reply when she tried her brother's cell phone, so she left a message on his direct office line. Next, she speed-dialed Ash, but the call went straight to voicemail.

Luc paced around the living room, his eyes wild. "We need to find Ash and hide him. Jones and his buddies may be searching for him now." He looked over at Iris. "Did you get through to him?"

Iris shook her head.

Luc fished his phone out of his back pocket and stabbed a button. "Angel? Is Ash OK after that fucking article? What? I can't understand you…Say that again…Oh my God, is he?…What hospital? I'm on my way."

"Tell me!"

Luc ran to the hall closet and grabbed his parka. "Ash was shot! I've got to get to Mass General now."

Iris was right behind him. "I'll drive."

★ ★ ★

Iris headed straight for the emergency drop-off. As Luc jumped out, she called, "I'll park, then come find you."

By the time she made it to the emergency waiting room, she spotted Luc and Angelique sitting together near a coffee machine. Her posture and expression showed that she was barely holding it together. Luc held her hand. When he saw Iris, he let go of the hand and motioned Iris over.

"What's happening?" Iris was out-of-breath. "How's Ash?"

Luc's voice was hoarse. "They're operating on him now. The nurse who came out told us he's got a partially collapsed lung."

*How dangerous is that? Can you breathe without help if your lung is partially collapsed?*

Tears streaked Angelique's cheeks. "Ash never hurt a fly, but someone tried to kill him!"

As Angelique began to cry again, Luc put an arm around her shoulder, murmuring, "Shh, shh, Angel. He's in the best hospital in the world. It's gonna be OK."

She looked up at him. "I made the ambulance come here. They wanted to go to a closer hospital, but I begged them to bring Ash here."

As the three of them sat staring at the floor, Iris' phone buzzed and danced in her pocket. Sterling's name was lit up on the screen. She moved toward the front entry and filled her brother in on Ash's condition. Sterling promised to find out what the Medford police were doing to apprehend the shooter.

They waited another half hour before double doors at the far end of the room opened and a tired-looking man in scrubs came out. "Family of Ashley Burke?"

Angelique and Luc approached him, Iris trailing behind.

"We're his parents, and I'm a nurse. Please give us the whole story," Angelique said.

The doctor answered with a quick, professional smile. "I'm Dr. Gregory Katz, the cardiovascular surgeon who just operated on your son. Ashley is doing fine. He's come through the surgery and is in recovery now. We removed a 9 mm bullet from his lower left lung. It struck the seventh rib and became lodged in the lung tissue, but didn't do much further damage. The bullet missed any other vital organs."

"Oh, thank God. Did he need a transfusion?" Angelique asked.

"We gave him five units of blood before the surgery."

"So, it didn't penetrate the abdominal cavity?"

"No, we performed a peritoneal lavage to check on that, but no blood was present. Ashley has two drains in his chest, but we'll be able to remove them in a few days. The important thing now is to keep his blood levels normal and to protect him from infection."

"When can we see him?" Luc asked.

"He'll be waking from the anesthesia in about an hour. Then, we'll take him to the I.C.U. and you can visit him there.

The police will need to interview him, as with all gunshot victims. Now, if you'll excuse me." Dr. Katz bowed his head and disappeared back through the double doors.

Angelique and Luc looked at each other and exhaled.

A thought struck Iris. "If a Medford policeman is going to interview Ash, how can we be sure it's not one of Jones' buddies? Ash may still be in danger." This earned Iris a pair of surprised looks.

Angelique turned to Luc. "She's right. Should we take shifts staying in his room?"

"Will they let us stay outside of visiting hours?" Luc asked.

"I'm dressed in my scrubs and nameplate. The other nurses will hopefully extend a professional courtesy in these circumstances."

"But how will you be able to fend off a cop or a hit man with a gun?" Iris asked. "Ash may need a bodyguard from Sterling's office."

"Or maybe I could call Ed, my father's old partner. He's retired, but he should have some idea about who we can trust from the Medford P.D."

Luc looked at his watch, then turned to Iris. "We're going to wait here for Ash to wake up, but you don't need to stick around." He led Iris toward the waiting room entry and gave her a quick hug. "Thanks, babe, for your support."

Iris looked blankly at Luc, turned and walked out of the hospital in a daze. *Thanks for my support? Had her lover just dismissed her?*

# Chapter 45

Luc finished a lengthy phone call to Ed while Angel paced at the other end of the waiting room, absorbed in a call of her own. He sat hunched in a chair trying to take in these new circumstances, but everything felt surreal. Up until the previous week, he hadn't heard Angel's name in years. But today, he'd held her in his arms as if no time had passed. A week ago, he'd had no clue he was a father. And now, he and Angel were sharing a nightmare. Someone was trying to kill their child. Is this what it meant to be a parent? To feel helpless and terrified?

Luc thought he should call his own mother to let her know that she had another grandchild, albeit a grown one. Would she be disappointed in him—that he hadn't even known about his son and been there in the way he should have?

As Angel crossed the room and came back into earshot, he heard her say, "Bruno needs to make this right. He promised he would." Her words emerged staccato, as if she were biting them off.

Luc's hands fisted. He slowly relaxed them and waited for Angel to sit down. Then he lobbed out an observation. "Ash told me that you're still in touch with Bruno and Maggie."

Angel stiffened, her small face unresponsive. "Uh, huh," she said, as she began intently checking messages on her phone.

*Was Bruno involved in getting Ash shot? If that was the case, wasn't he entitled to be told about it? Why did Angel keep pushing him away just when he thought he was gaining her trust?*

"Luc!" a loud female voice broke through his thoughts. Raven ran toward them, wearing what looked like pajama bottoms below her jeans jacket even though it was the middle of the day. "Angelique, oh God, how is he? Iris told me what happened. I don't think my wheels touched the pavement between Providence and Boston."

Raven fell into a seat next to Angelique and the older woman explained Ash's medical status.

"Thank God he'll be OK." Raven rocked back and forth, her arms crossed. "Will the police go after Terry's father?"

Angelique's voice went dark with anger. "Fat chance."

Luc got out of his seat and squatted down in front of Angel so that his face was level with hers. He reached for her hands. "We're going to get the people responsible for this. Sterling is working on it and I called my father's partner from the Cambridge Police. We're going to put these guys away, Angel. But if there's anything you know about the shooting, you need to tell me."

She bit her lip, considering. "Bruno asked Ash for a favor last summer. Jamal was getting out of rehab and Ash was supposed to warn Terry not to deal any more drugs to Jamal. Ash might have used strong words when he delivered the message, but he never hurt Terry."

"OK. That at least clarifies that Ash wasn't trying to buy drugs from Terry," Luc said. "This puts things in a different light."

Raven jumped in. "Is that what the girlfriend was implying? Ash doesn't do heavy drugs."

Luc stood up. "Maybe Iris can get Buchanan to write a retraction in the paper. We need to think about how to get this information out there." He checked the time on his phone and headed to the reception desk to see if Ash had been moved to the I.C.U. He returned and reported, "We can go up now to see him. He's in Blake 12."

It took them a while to navigate the 3-dimensional labyrinth of Mass General's various wings and elevator banks to locate Blake 12, then to find Ash's room.

The young man lay elevated in a hospital bed, eyes closed, the edge of a bandage on his chest visible above the sheets. He was hooked up to beeping monitors, and two plastic tubes drained watery pink liquid from under the bandages into a container. His arms rested on top of the covers.

Raven ran to him and stroked his hand. "Ash, baby?" she murmured. "Can you hear me?"

He groaned, opened his eyes, then smiled. "Raven."

"And your Mom's here, and Luc. You had us so worried. How are you doing?"

Angel took a seat at the bedside across from Raven, her hand covering her mouth. A tear rolled down her cheek. She touched the skin on his arm and rested her hand there.

Luc stood at the foot of the bed, feeling like an interloper. These women had an intimate connection with his son which he hadn't yet earned. He stared at the diluted blood draining out of his son's tubes. His biological son. Their shared blood. Someone had hurt his son. He felt a rush of love and protectiveness for this kid he barely knew. It was so far beyond anything he'd ever experienced before.

Ash's response sounded thick and slurred: "Feel like shit. Guy shot me?"

Angelique reassured him. "You're safe now. The doctor got the bullet out. You're going to heal completely." As if she was trying to convince herself.

Ash looked up at his mother. "m' I drugged? What'm I on?"

"You're still shaky from the surgery and the anesthesia. How's your throat? Let me get you some water."

After Angel bustled out to find a pitcher and glass, they heard a knock on the door frame. A large man with kind eyes stuck his head in. When he saw Luc, he entered.

Luc went over and embraced him. "Thanks for coming, Ed. This is my son, Ash."

A bear of a man in his sixties with gin blossoms on his cheeks flashed a look from Luc to Ash. He shook Ash's hand gently. "I'm Ed Rostow, your new bodyguard. I'm retired now, but your grandfather was my partner in the Cambridge Police Department for many years." He waved a Ken Follett paperback. "I'll be reading outside your door, and only hospital personnel or people you approve will get through. Us retired cops will trade shifts. We'll make sure you stay safe."

"Thanks," Ash said. "I hadn't…hadn't…"

"It's OK, just rest now." Luc turned to speak to Ed in a low voice. "Did you clear it with hospital security to withhold his name or room number?"

"Standard procedure with a gunshot victim." Ed patted Luc's shoulder. "But I touched base with them. No one's going to hurt Scott Cormier's grandson on my watch." With that, he grabbed a fiberglass chair and dragged it out of the room, closing the door behind him.

Ash looked vaguely in the direction of Luc. "My grandfather was a cop?"

# Chapter 46

Sean and Lawrence waited a block away from the Burke house, listening to the police scanner Sean had brought along. When they heard the report, "Drive-by shooting at 55 Maple Street… male civilian down with life-threatening injuries," Sean erupted. "The kid's not even dead! I knew this was a mistake." He floored the car. "I'm gonna get kicked off the force for helping you. Or worse, Romano's gonna chop off *my* fingers along with yours." His eyes met Lawrence's in the rear-view mirror. "You called in your marker, old Buddy, and I paid up. You're on your own now."

Sean drove silently the rest of the way back to the cottage, parked Lawrence's car in the garage and threw him the keys. "Take my advice and blow town. Medford just got twenty degrees hotter for you." He waved a brief salute as he stood by his own car. "And don't send me any post cards!"

When Lawrence had lowered the garage door and trudged inside, he slid the Smith & Wesson out from the back of his waistband. He emptied the chamber and laid the pistol on the

"""

kitchen counter. Sean was right—his ass was toast. He'd sent up a neon flare to Romano announcing his arrival back in town, just in case the guy had missed the memo about his release from prison.

Ash Burke had been what—twenty-five feet away? He'd aimed for the kid's heart, but, just at that moment, the kid had straightened up from reaching into his pocket and the bullet had hit too low. Lawrence had missed the money shot. He would check the local news before catching a flight out of the country, but he knew in his bones that Ash Burke was still alive. Before he left, he'd have to bury the gun in the backyard.

Lawrence headed for the bedroom and slid a suitcase out from under the bed. His plan was to use one of the fake passports from the heist to fly to La Paz, buy a sturdy SUV there, then drive down to Tarija, collecting intel along the way about local property and vineyards for sale. He'd brushed up on his high-school Spanish while in prison, but he'd have to pick up the dialect wherever he finally settled. He didn't want the locals talking about him behind his back or ripping him off.

Lawrence had gotten up to speed on using computers in the prison library and had been able to research all kinds of things. How many inmates knew that Bolivian wines were just starting to generate buzz internationally? Growing grapes in the high-altitude of the Bolivian mountains, although difficult, produced a red grape with a thicker skin and bolder flavor. He was confident he could amass vineyards rivaling the best of Chile and Argentina.

It was summer now in Bolivia, but Lawrence threw in all his new clothes. It would still be chilly at night in the mountains. He bet that the stars there shone extra-bright, so far away from any cities. A memory came to him of looking at the sky one night with a five-year-old Terry and pointing out a meteor shower. His son had been so excited.

Lawrence let himself fall onto the bed with a heavy 'oof'. How would he ever be able to look at that night sky in Bolivia without regret?

He had to try to finish this business, for Terry's sake, one more time.

# Chapter 47

Iris was biting into a roast-beef-and-tomato sandwich when she heard the chime of the apartment intercom. She recognized Ellie on the screen and buzzed her in.

Her friend was weighed down with paper grocery bags and a cloth tote over each shoulder. "I should have called first to make sure you were home." Ellie handed the bags to Iris.

"What are we doing with these?"

"You said I could store some things in your fridge and freezer for the party. Do you have enough space?"

Iris had completely forgotten about Ellie and Mack's annual Christmas open house that coming Saturday. "Sure, we'll find room."

"How's Ash doing?" Ellie asked, resting a tote on the counter.

"The doctor said he'll make a full recovery, thank God." Iris filled her in on the details.

"This is really bad. Was it the drug dealer's father who shot him?"

"I think so, or he got his crooked cop buddies to do it."

They emptied bags onto the counter. Iris consolidated the few things already in the freezer—three bags of frozen vegetables, coffee beans, five baggies of frozen herbs, and a bottle of vodka on the door. She arranged Ellie's boxes in the remaining space. The fridge was a tighter fit, but they methodically shuffled and stacked until they'd wedged in every one of Ellie's cartons and Tupperware containers.

Iris pointed to her half-eaten lunch. "Want a sandwich?"

"No, thanks. I've eaten."

They wandered over into the living room and sat down.

"Thanks for telling Raven about the shooting," Ellie said. "I'm sure Angelique was too freaked out to think of it."

"When we got to the hospital, Luc was giving her some heavy-duty comforting."

"Oh?"

"Then, after the doctor assured us that the surgery had gone well, and that Ash would be OK, Luc told me that I should head home to wait."

Ellie raised her eyebrows but said nothing.

Iris stared at her sandwich while she chewed, a bit too methodically. "What if he goes back to her?"

"He won't."

"Why not?"

"Because he loves you."

But Iris could see the concern on her friend's face. "Can I tell you something awful?"

"Of course."

"There was Ash fighting for his life, and all I was focused on were Luc and Angelique as this family unit worrying about their son." Iris lowered her voice. "It made me wish that Luc had never learned about his kid."

Ellie leaned forward and gave Iris' hand a squeeze. "That makes you human, Sweetie. Being human sucks sometimes."

Sheba peered up at Iris with mournful eyes, as if she'd been following the conversation. Iris reached down and scratched the ruff of the dog's neck.

The two women sat, locked in silence, before Ellie spoke again. "Do you think the Medford police will try very hard to find Terry's shooter? Won't the cops just assume it was a drug deal gone wrong? They might decide to look the other way."

"Sterling checked out the detective in charge, Rafael Gonzalez. He seems like a straight shooter. Sorry, bad pun."

"I don't understand why this Romano guy didn't go after Jones and the others after they'd learned they'd been robbed."

"I think it took them awhile to figure out who the robbers were. I wonder if they ever got any of their money back. One article I found said that most of the cash in the safety deposit boxes was illegal gambling proceeds that the Romano crime family was hiding from the IRS."

"Maybe they spread the word around the prison that they wanted Jones kept alive so he could lead them to his stash once he got out."

Iris reached for her laptop on the coffee table and slid it

close. "Let's see if we can find out what happened to the money." She typed in: *money recovered from 2004 Medford bank robbery?*

Ellie pointed to the third entry. "Oh, God." *Bank robber tortured.* The date of the entry was January 12, 2006:

**Police made a gruesome discovery today when they found the body of Medford Police Sergeant John McCarthy's mutilated body in the trunk of his car. Alongside the body were six cloth bags from the safety deposit boxes raided during the Medford Bank robbery the previous Labor Day weekend. Two stray gold coins and a small diamond, allegedly from the robbery, were found wedged in the corner of the trunk's upholstery. Police believe that members of organized crime discovered that McCarthy was one of the robbers and tortured him until he revealed where he had hidden his share of the proceeds.**

Ellie looked up. "The Romano crime family might have killed Terry as a warning to his father to give back their valuables."

"That makes a hell of a lot more sense than Ash killing Terry." Iris said.

"And then there are other drug buyers or rival dealers who might have had it in for the guy."

"Or maybe Terry's girlfriend wanted him out of the way and she's trying to divert attention onto Ash." Iris put her palms on the table and regarded Ellie. "Her accusation almost succeeded in getting Ash killed. In that case, the police could have closed the case with the convenient lie that Terry's murder had been solved."

"But how can we convince the police, and Jones Senior, that Ash didn't do it before the father can make another attempt?"

Iris frowned. "We need more information."

# Chapter 48

Lawrence peeked out through the living room curtains. No suspicious cars or pedestrians stood out from the low level of activity he'd expected to see on this Wednesday afternoon on the outskirts of Stoneham. Unless that elderly man bringing in a grocery bag from his car was not who he appeared to be, Lawrence was probably safe in the cottage for now.

He gave himself until Sunday to find the Burke kid again. He was required to check in with his parole officer on Tuesday. So, in case the police didn't already have a BOLO out for him after today's shooting episode, missing his parole appointment would surely set off alarm bells. Four days also seemed like the longest time he could hope to keep Romano from picking up his trail. But then again, he considered how long it took the Feds, much less the crime families, to track down Whitey Bulger. So, he'd have time to satisfy his conscience that he had done everything possible to make things right for Terry, then drive up to Montreal on Monday, at the latest. There, he'd buy a plane ticket to Mexico City, then continue flying south until he made it to La Paz.

How could he find out where Ash Burke was now? He'd missed his opportunity that morning to follow the ambulance, and Sean wasn't about to give him any more intel from police headquarters. Burke might be at any of the local hospitals and the Boston area had dozens of them. But, even if he tracked down the location, shooting victims were never registered under their real names. He'd have to get at this from another angle. Back when he was a detective, he'd look for a perp's "known confederates".

Lawrence sat on the edge of the sofa and flipped open his laptop. He needed to use his new computer chops to learn as much as possible about Burke. A Google search of the kid's name produced no hits. Lawrence hadn't had access to unsupervised internet use while he was in prison so, out of curiosity, he Googled himself. There were four pages of entries, all about the robbery. After skimming an unflattering *Boston Globe* article, he didn't bother with the rest.

He tried Facebook next, but Burke evidently didn't have a page. What else did kids use now—Twitter? He googled "what social media do college kids use now?" and got the responses: Snapchat, Tinder, Grindr, and Instagram. Since further study revealed that the first site made your messages disappear, and he was pretty sure that the next two were about finding sex partners, he went on to Instagram. Bingo—Ashley Burke had an Instagram account, and it was open to the public. Lawrence scrolled through a bunch of weird paintings and photos of gritty street scenes. Depressing. He spotted a shot of Burke with an arm around an older woman with a clear family resemblance. Must be the mother. Man, she was a knock-out. It could prove helpful to know what she looked like, although hanging around her house at this point was a no-go. Romano and the police were probably tripping over each other just waiting for Lawrence to return there.

On the next page, an artsy-looking young woman wearing a long scarf was riding a bike. He found several more of her, including one showing her with Burke. From the looks they were giving each other, she was definitely his girlfriend. Very pretty. He tried not to compare her to Clorise, his son's girlfriend. Unfortunately, Instagram didn't tell you the names that corresponded with the people so he wouldn't be able to track her down that way. But wait. If he clicked on the cycling picture, he saw an icon of Burke's face next to the words "My Raven—always in flight." Below that comment, he saw an icon of the girl next to the name ravenmckenzie and her response, "Maybe I'll let you fly with me." Was that the girl's name, Raven McKenzie? Who names a girl "Raven"?

Lawrence was beginning to get the knack of this. He clicked on the girl's icon and was sent directly to her Instagram page. She had far more followers than her boyfriend, 2,384 of them to be exact, and listed "Painter" under her heading, as the Burke kid did. Lots of images of wild, colorful paintings filled her site, but she had more shots of college-studenty-types as well. A recent photo showed her with an older but much shorter woman with curly red hair, standing in front of a big house with a wreath on the door. The comment read "Getting prepped for our annual Christmas party." Lawrence checked the date. It was posted the previous weekend. In the responses, Elliemckenzie's icon wrote back, "But will it all be ready by Saturday?" He clicked on the mother's icon, and her site identified her as an architectural historian. He studied her page until he picked out in her comments the phrase "We Cantabridgians…", the odd designation for the inhabitants of Cambridge.

It took little time to put these clues together. He looked up Ellie McKenzie in Cambridge through the online white pages and learned that Ellie, Mack and Raven lived at 27 Arlington Street. He knew that they were having a Christmas party on Saturday. The only question was whether Raven's boyfriend would be recovered enough from the gunshot wound Lawrence had given him that morning to attend.

# Chapter 49

Later that evening, street lights were glinting along Mass Avenue and pedestrians were trudging home, heads bent down against a fine drizzle. A thin fog blurred the outlines of the low-rise storefronts across the street. Iris turned away from her living room window and tried calling Luc but, once again, he wasn't picking up. His phone must be turned off. Her eyes felt sore and gritty from too much staring out into the growing dark.

As she slid her phone back into her pocket, she heard tapping at the door of the apartment's internal stair that connected to the restaurant below. She descended to find a worried-looking Claire, the Paradise' young Maître d', waiting on the far side of the door.

"Sorry to bother you, Iris, but have you seen Luc? He's not answering his cell."

"I think he's still at the hospital, a family emergency. Anything I can help with?"

Claire, who doubled as a Bikram yoga teacher during the

day, tugged at the spaghetti strap of her tight-fitting black dress. "He texted me earlier that Arnold would be cooking tonight, but I just got a last-minute table request, and I suspect it's the James Beard guy again. He used the same name, and he stuck to a single glass of wine with dinner last time, which is sort of the tip-off. We had a cancellation, so I fit him in, but I thought Luc might want to cook, given the high stakes." Claire paused to take a breath. "It could be our last chance to make a good impression before the judges decide on this year's winners."

It had been hours since Iris had left Luc back at Mass General. He'd definitely want to do the honors for the James Beard inspector himself. "I'll text him about it. That's all we can do. And wish everyone good luck tonight."

Iris returned upstairs and resumed pacing back and forth in the living room. Was Luc still at the hospital? His son had just been shot. Had Jones Senior discovered Luc's connection to Ash and hurt him too? She considered calling the nurse's station when the intercom buzzed.

She didn't recognize the large man who faced the doorbell camera, but raced down the stairs hoping that he might have some news about Luc.

"Hi, I'm Ed Rostow," The twinkly eyed man said. "I was partners with Luc's Dad many years ago. You must be Iris. I was hoping to speak with Luc."

*Join the club.* Iris tried not to show her disappointment as she invited him upstairs.

"Luc has told me so much about you." Ed continued. "I've known Luc since he was a baby."

"He's told me about you too. It's nice to meet you, Ed. Luc isn't here now. I think he's still at the hospital."

"I just came from there. He asked me and several of us other retired cops to guard his son's room. I saw Luc briefly, but he left after an hour. I figured I'd catch up with him after my shift was over."

"I'm not really sure where he is right now." A tiny pain throbbed behind Iris' left eye. "Let me text him that you're here. I'm sure he'll want to thank you for watching over Ash. Can I get you a beer or a glass of wine?"

"Nice place. A beer would be great, thanks." Ed followed her into the living room and sat down, looking around.

Iris sent off a text and brought in an IPA from the kitchen fridge. "How's the patient? Has Ash had any more visitors?"

Ed took a sip and leaned back. "Well, his girlfriend and mother stayed the whole time. They're probably still there. Like I said, Luc left a few hours ago. A nurse came in a few times and his doctor checked on him. But don't worry—I made sure those people were all legit."

"Luc must be relieved to have you and the others there for protection," Iris said. "I still can't believe that someone actually tried to kill Ash this morning. Did Luc fill you in on who we think was behind it?"

Ed set down his beer can on the coffee table and nodded. "I remember the robbery. Scott Cormier and I took our vow to protect and defend seriously. Scott lost his life doing it. But that scumbag, Lawrence Jones, was a dirty cop and arrogant enough to rob a bank, stealing money from the Mob, for God's sake. And now, when I think he might be the one behind trying to kill Scott's grandson, it makes my blood boil."

"Did you know much about the Medford Police Department back then? Was it known for corruption?"

"Those inside the thin blue line generally keep their dirty laundry hidden. It wasn't until the three cops were exposed as the safe deposit box robbers that Medford PD had to step up and deal with the problem. I have a friend from the Cambridge PD who transferred there when his family moved. He says the force did a major clean-up post-2006, but that there are still more than a few bent ones. And it doesn't help the city's image that one of the Romano crime family, Frankie Romano, still lives in the Fulton Heights area of town. It sounds like Ash may have gotten himself in the middle of a war between Jones and Romano."

"Any ideas about how can we get him out of the line of fire?"

Ed shrugged. "Find out who actually killed Terry Jones."

"Can't they use forensic evidence or trace the bullet?"

"It's not so easy. I called my Medford cop friend from the hospital and he said that Terry Jones' body had been moved from the actual murder site several months before it was found. Then someone set a fire to burn whatever evidence might have remained. Unless the crime scene guys get lucky or the gun shows up, it's gonna be tough to ID the killer."

"Meanwhile, the Medford police view Ash as a convenient suspect."

"Detective Gonzalez must be under a lot of pressure from the Chief of Police now that the Globe has picked up the story. He needs someone quick to perp-walk in front of the cameras, at least to put the investigation into a holding pattern while the publicity dies down. I'm not saying this would happen, but Gonzalez could twist the evidence and implicate Ash on these very slim pretexts. He has the power to do that. Then, when Ash is inside the lockup, maybe stuck in there with a bunch of violent felons, Gonzalez might find himself handed a confession. That or Ash gets out and is used as bait to flush out the real murderer."

Iris swallowed. "I thought that Gonzalez was a straight shooter. You're saying he might let an innocent kid get hurt just to close his case?"

Ed sighed. "I've seen that happen, and worse. But that's why we need to make sure that Gonzalez never gets Ash into the Medford lockup."

"Why don't the cops go after Romano? He probably killed Terry to get his father to turn over the robbery money the minute he got out of jail. Shouldn't Gonzalez be pulling hard on that thread?"

"For the most part, Frankie Romano's guys are professionals, and they wouldn't leave a body behind for the cops to find, only to have to return to burn evidence. And I'm pretty sure that Jones Senior's gone to ground. Romano's guys must be pretty much desperate to get their hands on him."

"But Terry was a low-life drug dealer. He might have had arguments with other customers or his competition."

"The girlfriend's story about Ash and Terry getting into a fight right before he disappeared is circumstantial, but it makes Ash look guilty. It seems to have convinced Jones Senior who, if he had any sense, should be right now skipping town to get away from Romano, instead of hanging around trying to avenge his son's murder. That means that Jones, Romano and Gonzalez might all be trailing our boy."

"So, I guess Ash needs to hide? For how long?"

"Until Medford PD can draw out the real killer or until Romano can find Jones."

Iris sat up straighter. "That's right. If Jones gets taken off the field, there'd be no more danger to Ash."

"Except now that the media has picked up the story, Gonzalez still needs to produce Terry's murderer."

# Chapter 50

Iris was putting her dinner dishes into the dishwasher when she heard a key in the lock downstairs. She could tell by the sound of Luc's heavy tread on the stairs that he was exhausted, and the sight of his face as he entered the kitchen confirmed that. His shaggy blond hair stood on end as if he'd been running his hands through it all afternoon. Iris wrapped him in a hug.

He slid an arm around her back, then pulled away. "Sorry I didn't answer your texts. I was at my mother's. It got a bit…emotional."

"You told her about Ash? How'd she take it?"

"She said that no matter how Ash's existence had come about, it was not his fault and she would try to love him just as much as Mary's girls." Luc's expression expressed scorn more eloquently than any words could have managed.

Iris let out a low whistle.

Luc opened the freezer, and a large Tupperware container slipped out at him. He grabbed it mid-air, peered at it, registered the packed interior and looked quizzically at Iris.

"Ellie's Christmas party. She needed to store some things."

Luc shoved the box back in and lifted the vodka bottle out of the door pocket. Iris handed him a glass, and he filled it with ice, then with the frozen vodka before heading into the living room.

"She made me go to Mass with her." Luc sank onto the sofa and unbuttoned his jacket.

Iris walked over and sat beside him. "Did she make you do the confession thing in the little booth?"

He eyed her over his glass. "Not this time."

Iris leaned forward. "Oh—did you get my text about the possible James Beard Inspector?"

Luc threw his head back and closed his eyes. "I'm not going down there now. I'd just blow their rhythm. Arnold can handle it. It's been a long fucking day."

"Why don't you go lie down? Wait—did you have dinner?"

"I ate at my mother's place."

Iris could see the tension in his jaw and the faint lines bracketing his eyes. She was close enough to feel the heat of him and was tempted to run her fingertips along the bare skin of his collarbone visible in the V of his sweater.

He sat up and gave her a grim smile. "There's something I need to talk to you about."

She felt a chill, as if a foreign spirit had just entered the room and settled down between them.

"This doesn't seem fair to you, but I can't think of any other solution."

Iris steeled herself to hear his next words. *Get on with it.*

"I never expected to run into Angel again and to learn that we had a kid."

She felt nauseous. So he wanted to talk about Angelique. She stared miserably at the floor.

"But now that I know about Ash, I want to protect him. Seeing him lying in that hospital bed, wounded and helpless, it brought out these…feelings."

*Wait—this was about Ash?*

"I spoke with his doctor. Ash needs to stay in the hospital for a few more days until they can remove his tubes. Then he can be discharged, but he'll need to take it easy. Here's the thing. I doubt that Jones is going to give up trying to find him, so Ash will need to hide someplace that Jones doesn't know about."

Iris suddenly got it. "You want Ash to stay here with us?"

"It's a big ask. You're at home during the day trying to work. And I'm not sure how long he would need to hide here. What do you think?"

She could have laughed with relief. "Sure. Of course he can stay here. He can sleep on the pull-out sofa in my office."

Luc sighed and settled back again. "You're a real trouper, Iris."

At those words, her uneasiness returned. Iris didn't want to be seen as a girl scout. She wanted Luc to think of her with unquestionable passion. She wanted to make him forget that Angelique ever existed.

# Chapter 51

Angelique was exhausted by the time the Uber dropped her at Maggie's front door, several blocks from her own house. Her mascara was smeared and her eyes felt swollen.

Maggie hugged her. "Oh, God."

They held on to each other for a moment in the front hall before moving into the small living room.

"I almost lost him," Angelique said as she collapsed into a chair.

"But he'll be fine—right?"

"I don't know. The doctor says his lungs will recover. But someone tried to kill him. How will he ever be the same?"

Maggie pushed her hair back from her face and met Angelique's eyes straight on. "This is my fault."

"What? No, it's not. What are you talking about?"

"We should've spoken up sooner, Bruno and I. But I never thought this would blow back onto Ash."

These words made no sense to Angelique. Her mind was numb.

"I know who killed Terry," Maggie said. "I've known since last summer."

"You *know*? You mean Frankie Romano?"

"No." Maggie bit her lip. "Bruno shot him."

"*Bruno*? Why would he shoot Terry?"

"He caught him selling drugs to Jamal."

It took a minute for Angelique to take this in. "Tell me what happened."

"Back in August, the night after Ash warned Terry to stay away, Jamal phoned him and Terry came over to our house. He climbed in Jamal's window in the basement and Bruno caught the asshole weighing out meth on Jamal's bed, brazen as that."

"Unbelievable!" Angelique's head fell back against the chair and she closed her eyes.

"Bruno went crazy. He got his gun out of our bedroom closet and shot the bastard while he was trying to crawl out the window."

The horror Angelique felt quickly turned to anger. When she was able to speak, her voice shook. "You knew this the whole time? While the police were questioning Ash? After that animal, Jones got out of prison?"

"Wait—please listen." Maggie leaned over to touch Angelique's arm, but she pulled it back. "No one could have predicted that someone would shoot Ash."

Angelique stared at her.

Maggie looked miserable. "The three of us were going to bury Terry in the woods next to that old warehouse, but we

were too tired to dig a big hole. You remember how weak
Bruno was by last summer. So we shoved Terry's body down
the foundation of the warehouse chimney and covered it with
leaves. We figured the corpse would decompose before anyone
found it. No one's used that property in ages. It never occurred
to us that someone would buy it to develop, much less Ash."

"So you set the fires? Did you even consider that Ash might
have been inside?"

"I made absolute sure he wasn't. We needed to get rid of
any DNA we might have left behind." Maggie's eyes were
pleading. "Jamal waited until Ash and the architect left the
building, then credit carded his way in the back door to smash
the sprinkler box. We figured Ash would get a big insurance
payout after the building burned down and that would be a
good thing. He was in my restaurant when the fire was set, so
he had an alibi for the time. I didn't know that Ash didn't have
any insurance on it."

"Don't you understand? You let him take the fall for Bruno
murdering some kid. The paper has made Ash out to be a
killer, mixed up with a drug dealer. He'll never live that down.
You put a target on my son's back. He could have died!"

Tears rolled down Maggie's cheeks. "You know I never
meant any of that to happen. I love you like a sister. Ash is like
my nephew."

"Then why didn't you tell me all this last August?"

"That would have made you an accessory."

"Like we haven't shared secrets before?"

Maggie nodded dully. Her face was expressionless, blank. "When you told me last night that the police had brought Ash in for questioning, I went to see Detective Gonzalez and let him know what really happened."

Angelique's eyebrows rose. "I've been checking the news on my phone all day. I haven't heard anything about a confession." Her face sobered. "Or didn't Gonzalez believe you?"

"I don't know. Maybe he thought we were trying to get Ash off the hook. I said that Bruno tossed his gun into the Mystic River from the Harvard Avenue bridge. Gonzalez is going to get some officers to dredge the river to look for it. If it's where I told him, he said he'd call a press conference."

Angelique squeezed her eyes shut.

Maggie continued, "This morning, Gonzalez came to our house to take Bruno's statement. The Hospice worker confirmed that his illness is terminal. Bruno said he disposed of the body himself, that Jamal and I weren't involved. Still, I'm sure we'll face some sort of charges." She looked toward Angelique for sympathy but found none. "As soon as Gonzalez announces that Bruno was the one who killed Terry, Jones will leave Ash alone."

Angelique stopped and faced her friend. "A little late for that, don't you think? What if the cops never find the gun? What if they decide that Ash threw it there and Bruno's taking the fall because he's about to die?"

Maggie winced at Angelique's bluntness. A moment passed, but the tension between them didn't dissipate.

Angelique rose and hefted her satchel strap over her shoulder. The memory of all the things she'd lost due to her friendship with Maggie and Bruno hit her like a slap. "It was one thing when you two were just blowing up *my* life, but now you're doing it to Ash as well!" She stalked over to the front door, banging it on her way out.

# Chapter 52

Maggie sagged against the chair at the thought of her oldest friend's anger. Justified anger. Twenty years ago, an innocent request from Maggie had caused Angelique to be wrenched apart from the handsome boy she loved and whose child she was carrying, a child who would spend his earliest years without a father. She remembered the many nights she'd heard Angelique crying herself to sleep in the next room of her aunt's small house in Medford, and the years when Angelique refused to date anyone because her heart still belonged to Luc Cormier. It was a wonder her friend had ever forgiven her and Bruno. Sure, part of it was desperation, a need to band together for survival as they raised their bi-racial sons together in a distinctly unfriendly world. But Angelique had always had a loyal, forgiving nature.

Now Maggie was pushing up against the far edge of that nature. It was one thing for Maggie and Bruno to sidetrack so many of Angelique's opportunities in life—a full scholarship to Berkeley, a loving relationship, the possibility of an intact home for her son. But for them to have put Ash in such extreme danger, no matter how unintentionally, had been going too far. Ash could have died today.

Maggie's eyes travelled to a framed photo of her own family on the mantlepiece. Taken several years ago, Bruno looked strong and healthy. Jamal's addiction was still in its early stages, so he appeared relatively fine—scowling, but he'd been a teenager then. She herself looked a lot better, before the constant stress of running the restaurant had etched deepening lines in her forehead and around her eyes. She felt hypnotized by the image. Her family of three.

Within a few hours, it would be just the two of them. Maggie and her damaged son.

One of the reasons that Angelique had dropped by tonight was to give Bruno his nightly shot of morphine. She'd volunteered to take on this task since her return from Haiti because she knew that Maggie had always been squeamish around needles. That had probably saved her from the hard drugs that had ensnared so many around her. The visiting hospice aide gave Bruno his shots during the day. Angelique had either forgotten or decided to blow off that chore tonight.

What Angelique hadn't known was that Maggie and Bruno had a different plan for tonight. Bruno had confessed to Terry's murder, but he had no intention of spending his last days in a prison infirmary. Maggie had asked the hospice aide to leave her extra morphine, "in case Bruno took a turn for the worse."

Maggie moved slowly down the hallway, listening at the

basement door for the usual sound of Jamal watching TV. Her own medicine cabinet was the next stop. The bottle of Ambien now held thirty tablets, the result of several months of stockpiling. She entered the spare bedroom and waited for her eyes to adjust to the low light of a table lamp. Bruno's dinner of chicken and rice sat untouched on a side tray table. Her husband had once been a vital, strapping man who drew people to him—not the skeleton he was now. She advanced closer and perched on the edge of the hospital bed. Was he asleep?

His eyes flickered open and he looked at her. "Is Angelique going to help us?"

Maggie shook her head. She hadn't told him that Ash had been shot that morning or that Angelique had spent the day at the hospital. No need to make him feel any more guilty than he already did. "I'm going to do it. We've involved her in too much already."

She found the medical lock-box propped on a chair and undid its combination lock. It took a few minutes to line up all ten of the syringes in the bag alongside a bottle of tea-colored liquid on top of the bureau. She took the bottle of Ambien from her pocket and shook out the tablets onto a saucer sitting next to the bottle.

Bruno looked at the number of hypodermic needles with alarm, then raised his eyes to hers in silent question.

Maggie smiled at him. "The time is right, my love."

She crushed the pills thoroughly with the back of a spoon, then swept the powder into a glass of water. Sitting beside

Bruno, cradling his head, she helped him sip the milky contents. Throughout the twenty minutes it took for him to complete drinking, she sang to him in a wavering soprano. First, "Love Has No Pride", followed by "My Baby Just Cares For Me", and ending with Jimmy Cliff's classic, "Many Rivers To Cross". After finishing the last verse, she gazed down at his now-relaxed face and asked quietly, "You scared?"

"No, baby. I'm ready for the tunnel and the white light."

Now came the tricky part. Maggie stood and inserted the needle of the first syringe through the rubber cap of the morphine bottle, inverted it and pulled back the plunger, ignoring the halfway point indicated on the side. She filled the second syringe, repeating until all ten were ready.

"I love you," he rasped quietly and reached out for her hand.

Maggie squeezed his hand back, "I've always loved you, Bruno."

Their eyes met—holding for a long second, before he pulled his hand back and the moment was gone.

She leaned over him, flicked the barrel of the syringe once to remove air bubbles and inserted the first full load of morphine between his gum and his lip. Twice the amount prescribed, but not lethal. He stared at the ceiling. Sweat slicked his brow.

"Keep going," he mumbled.

She followed with the next dose, watching as his pupils got large and his breathing became rattled. Over the time it took to administer all ten doses, his pupils shrank down to the size of pencil points. There were long breaks between his breaths and his eyes drooped to half-mast.

She sat with him until she no longer heard a breath for some time. His eyes were now completely closed. She reached for his bony wrist and felt no pulse. Gradually, her shoulders unclenched and she could breathe again. But her face was wet and her vision was blurry. She realized that she was crying.

# Chapter 53

Iris had spent Thursday trying to make her home office presentable as an improvised guest room. She'd stashed drawings away in her flat files, swept desk clutter into drawers, and returned catalogs to her bookcase. But she decided to leave the dozen inspirational images she'd pinned on the wall around her computer. Maybe they would provide Ash with some welcome visual stimulation after two days of being cooped up in a dull, sterile hospital room.

On Friday afternoon, Iris held the door open as Luc helped Ash up the stairs. The young patient looked terrible—weak and in pain, but Angelique had insisted that her son would risk getting an infection if he stayed any longer in the hospital. She'd agreed to hiding Ash in Luc and Iris' apartment, but only after Luc promised to follow her four detailed pages of handwritten care instructions.

At the top of the stairs, Sheba waddled over to greet Ash while Luc consulted Angelique's mandatory manual. "My marching orders say I'm supposed to take you directly to your bed." He dropped the stapled sheets on the kitchen counter along with a bottle of pills. "Do you want to lie down or would you rather sit propped up on the living room sofa?"

Ash gave him a surprised smile. "The sofa, thanks. I've been going stir-crazy lying in bed."

Luc swung a large duffle bag down from his shoulder, then maneuvered Ash carefully onto the couch. "Here's the stuff your mother brought to the hospital. Clothes, books, and a sketch pad. Your phone's in there too. How 'bout something to eat? I made some mushroom soup. It's vegan."

Ash closed his eyes and sighed. "Perfect."

Iris carried over a glass of water and set down a pill within reach. "Time for another Percocet."

Once the pain pill kicked in, Ash revived enough to finish off a large bowl of soup. He lay back against the cushions, Sheba nestled at his feet.

Luc checked his watch. "If you're OK, I'm going downstairs to prep for dinner. My backup chef, Allegra, is cooking tonight as well, so if you need me, just have Iris call. I'll check on you when I get a chance but Iris will be over there in the kitchen baking in case you need anything."

"No worries. Thanks for everything." Ash fished a set of ear buds out of the duffel bag and settled down to rest.

Iris tucked a duvet over him, then retreated to the kitchen to work on the pair of Bûche de Noëls she'd promised to make for Ellie's party. She cracked four egg whites into a stainless steel bowl and turned the Kitchenaid mixer on high. It was strange having Ash stay here. She still thought of him as her client or her goddaughter's boyfriend. But now he would be part of their family.

Two hours later, Iris scored the Bûches' chocolate icing with a fork to make it resemble the bark of a fallen branch and stood back to inspect them. *Do they look like turds?* She plopped the meringue mushrooms she'd made earlier around the edges of the cakes, covered them with foil and shoehorned the plates into the refrigerator.

The living room was silent except for Sheba's gentle snoring. Iris tiptoed around the sofa to check on whether Ash was asleep. At the movement, Sheba awoke and scrambled to her feet. Ash's eyes opened.

"Sorry," Iris whispered. "I didn't mean to wake you."

He pushed himself into a seated position and rubbed his eyes. "That's OK. If I sleep too long now, I'll be up all night."

"How do you feel?"

Ash shifted his torso slightly to either side. "My ribs are still pretty sore." He picked up the air buds that had fallen onto his pillow. "Thanks for taking me in. I hope I'm not putting you in any danger."

"No, this should all blow over soon."

Ash scratched his head. "I don't understand why Detective Gonzalez won't release a statement saying that Bruno confessed to killing Terry. My mother says that he wants to find the gun first before he'll take Bruno and Maggie at their word. But that still leaves *me* in Jones' sights."

Iris sat down across from him. "Hopefully he's wised up and left the country by now. Or word leaked out that someone else confessed to Terry's murder. It must have been a shock for you—learning that someone you actually knew had been the shooter."

"Once Mom explained the circumstances, I can't say that I blame Bruno. He was just trying to protect Jamal. And Maggie came forward and told the cops what really happened as soon as she learned that I was considered a serious suspect."

"Sounds like your two families are pretty tight."

"We are. And I can't believe that Bruno has really passed away. Maggie visited me in the hospital on Thursday to tell me. Luckily, it sounds like he went peacefully in his sleep. I want to go to his Memorial Service on Sunday. I just hope that Jones has been captured by then. By Frankie Romano or the cops—I don't care who nails him." Ash coughed and went on. "Speaking of police, can you tell me anything about about Luc's father? What kind of guy was he?"

"I don't know that much. He died when Luc was in high school. He and Ed were partners in the Vice division and Scott got killed by a drug dealer, I think."

"Right…Scott. Is Dottie his wife?"

"Yes, how did you know her name? Did someone mention it at Thanksgiving?"

"A couple of years ago, I took down a poetry book from our bookcase and a card fell out. It said 'Congratulations' on the front and inside, 'Dear Angelique, This is to help out while you're at Berkeley. Love, Dottie and Scott.'" Ash's face looked sheepish. "I probably shouldn't have read it."

Iris didn't bother to mask her surprise.

Ash glanced away uncertainly. "Do you know what 'while you're at Berkeley' meant? Does it refer to the music college in Boston?"

Iris was in over her head. She didn't want to make Ash feel like his existence had kept his mother from a promising college career. She wasn't even sure if that *was* the reason Angelique never enrolled at the University of California at Berkeley. Damn the woman. Why couldn't she be straight with Luc about what had happened?

"You should ask Luc. He can answer your questions and tell you all about your grandparents."

# Chapter 54

That night, Luc helped Ash to the guest room where a pull-out couch had been made up for him. After Luc closed the door, Ash looked around. His head felt woozy, but he wasn't ready to sleep again. This room must be Iris' office. A niche between a pair of bookshelves contained a desk with a wall of brightly colored images above. He shuffled over to take a closer look and sank into her desk chair. His eyes went to a black-and-white sketch on yellow tracing paper of a modern-looking house set on cascading levels. It was done with a loose, confident style. Had Iris designed and drawn this? There's always something revealing about one visual artist inspecting another's drawings, seeing their gesture, their "hand".

Next to the sketch was a print that he recognized as an early Helen Frankenthaler painting. He knew it was called *Seven Types of Ambiguity,* one of her first soaked canvas Abstract Expressionist paintings. It was one of his favorites, too. He drank in the shades of celadon and red, the brush movements and the spacial depth. His attention moved on to a postcard of a building by a Mexican architect that he remembered from a college survey course. Brightly painted walls in saturated reds, purples and whites intersected in a cubist pattern. A photograph above it also looked familiar. It was a cathedral skewed on an angle built inside a huge Mosque. Wasn't this in Spain? The arches and columns established a grid with the church's position deviating from the grid.

Finally, someone was speaking his language! After days in the hospital listening to beeping monitors and doctors spouting medical-speak, he was back in a visual world where shape, color, and light mattered.

Ash reluctantly drifted back toward the bed and climbed in gingerly, trying to find a comfortable position, but his mind was too keyed up for sleep. He wanted to start creating again. Was he strong enough to sit upright to paint? Maybe his mother could send over a stretched canvas and some tubes of paint. What about the idea of a painting based on this inspiration board with Iris in the center in some kind of stylized form? After all, Ash firmly believed that what one chose intentionally to look at every day became part of who you were.

He rolled painfully onto his other side. He'd thought of Iris as his architect or as Raven's godmother. Now what was she? Some kind of step-mother? Bizarre. And Luc? Ash couldn't believe that, now that he didn't need him anymore, his biological father had turned up. Damn. Why hadn't Luc been around when Ash was a little kid and desperately wanted to

have a father like the other kids did to play with him and teach
him things? Tavis Burke had come along when Ash was six,
and he'd been great. But Ash could have used Luc before that,
in the years when his mother had to work so hard at nursing
school, then at the hospital. *And what the hell did Luc expect
from him now?*

Even through the Percocet haze, his bullet wound ached.
Someone had tried to kill him! He still couldn't wrap his head
around it. The memory of it kept flashing through his mind.
The sound first. Like a loud *pop*. Then the searing pain. He'd
collapsed in the driveway, the sound of his mother's screaming
reaching him from far, far away.

Ash hadn't seen the shooter or his car, but he knew it had
to have been Jones. At the thought of the man, he could feel the
hair lifting on his arms. Was the guy still searching for him?
Could he trace him to this apartment? How would Ash ever
defend himself in the shape he was in?

# Chapter 55

I ris woke up Saturday morning to the sound of slow footsteps coming from somewhere in the apartment. Confused, she turned to Luc lying asleep next to her and shook him lightly. "I hear someone."

He opened his eyes and lay still, listening. "Ash." He rolled back over and closed his eyes again.

*Oh, yeah.* Iris grabbed a robe from a hook on the bathroom door. When she reached the kitchen, she saw him in pajama bottoms and a T-shirt with bulky bandages visible underneath.

Ash was staring at Luc's complicated Italian espresso maker. "I feel like I should be able to figure this mother out."

"You'd need an advanced degree in Industrial Design. I'll make you a cup." Iris flipped on some switches and took down two cups from the cabinet. "You sleep OK?"

"Compared to the hospital, it was amazing."

While Ash drifted to the dining table, holding his coffee cup in both hands, Iris tossed several slices of sourdough bread into the toaster. She joined him several minutes later carrying a tray containing plates of toast, jam, smashed avocado sprinkled with seeds, and two glasses of fresh-squeezed orange juice. "Luc's sleeping in. He's always wiped out after cooking on Friday or Saturday nights.

Ash reached for a plate. "This looks chill but don't let me mess up your schedule. You should sleep in too."

"I never can." Iris trotted down to the first floor, and came back up with the *Boston Globe* in its blue plastic bag. She unwrapped it and went straight to the Metro section, looking for any announcements about Bruno's confession. She found no mention today of what Budge had taken to calling the *Medford chimney murder*, but couldn't help wondering if the reporter felt any guilt at all about repeating Clorise's unsubstantiated accusation, then learning that Ash had gotten shot soon after. Probably not.

Looking over at the fragile young man sipping coffee across from her, intent on reading something on his phone, she understood what Luc meant about feeling protective of Ash.

An hour later, Luc dragged himself out of bed and wandered in to join them. Iris and Ash were in the living room having an animated discussion.

Ash appeared wan, propped up against the sofa cushions, but his eyes were animated. "I thought I was the only one who loved Frankenthaler's early stain paintings."

From her chair, Iris leaned forward. "Have you ever tried her technique? Letting the oil paint soak into a canvas primed with turpentine?"

"Yeah. It's wild. The paint is as translucent as watercolor but the pigment is so intense it almost vibrates."

"She achieves so much depth. I've always thought they were brilliant. But, of course, in the 1950s and 60s, her stuff got totally eclipsed by Morris Louis' Veil series even though he based them on her work."

"Typical."

"Totally."

# Chapter 56

Lawrence had lost his inside track on information about Gonzalez' investigation when Sean bailed, but there'd been nothing on the news about the cops arresting Burke. Just like he'd predicted, Gonzalez wasn't going to bust his hump trying to bring in the murderer of a drug dealer.

So Saturday found Lawrence huddled in his car on Arlington Street. The hardest thing about surveillance of the McKenzie house was the parking situation. Damn Cambridge and their Resident Permit only street parking. Lawrence had no idea when the party was supposed to start. He guessed that it might be an afternoon gig, so he'd gotten there at eleven. But Lawrence could only find a parking space several houses away. And then, just before noon, he'd had to pull out and drive around the block to avoid getting ticketed by a Traffic & Parking cop. When he returned to the street, a space only one house away had opened up. After he pulled into the spot, he checked in the mirror to make sure that his wool cap and sunglasses gave him an adequate disguise. Hopefully, old gray

Camrys were ubiquitous enough that Burke wouldn't recognize this one if he'd glimpsed it on Wednesday.

Since he might have to wait for hours, he'd brought a book, an old Robert Crais mystery that he'd found at the cottage. He was getting caught up in the story, all the while chewing absently on a turkey sandwich, and almost missed seeing a couple walking up to the front door of #27, a tall blond guy and a good-looking brunette with long hair, each carrying covered plates.

Over the next hour he saw a steady stream of guests entering the house, most arriving on foot. It began to look like a clown car emptying in reverse. Everyone the McKenzies knew must be in there, but he'd seen no sign of the Burke kid. Maybe he *had* died in the hospital. But Lawrence had seen the girl, Raven-from-Instagram, come to the door a few times to greet party-goers. She'd looked way too cheerful to have just lost a boyfriend.

In his rear-view mirror, Lawrence noticed a dark-green Subaru creeping down the street. The woman driving seemed to be checking house numbers. When she got closer, he looked over and recognized her. Ash Burke's mother. Thank you, Instagram. *She* wouldn't be partying if her son's health hadn't improved. The kid must be stashed away somewhere she considered safe—possibly inside this house? The mother parked in the McKenzie driveway and walked to the front door. She was immediately swallowed up into the festivities.

Should he follow her after she left or was Ash Burke inside?

Lawrence was running out of time. His gun was stored in the glove compartment, ready to finish the job he'd started. He couldn't blow it again.

The mother stayed at the party for less than an hour and came out accompanied by the first couple to arrive. They all walked around to her Subaru and she opened the trunk. The blond guy took out a large shopping bag, handing it to the brunette. Then he retrieved a large white canvas, *the thing artists like Ash Burke painted on.* Lawrence lowered his window in time to hear the brunette say, "He's been dying to get back to work."

*Dying indeed.*

The front door of the house opened again, and Christmas music emanated out into the street. The girlfriend, Raven, rushed toward the group, calling out to the brunette, "Tell him I'll FaceTime him when the party's over." That clinched it. Lawrence would follow the couple instead of the mother. The four of them said their goodbyes, and the mother got into her car. The couple started walking down the hill, the canvas under the man's arm.

Luckily, the direction of the one-way street allowed him to trail them. At the bottom of the hill, they turned right onto Mass Ave. He hovered for a minute at the corner to allow them to get out in front of him, then crept behind. After two blocks, they turned into the driveway of a large old-fashioned house with a sign over the front porch proclaiming it to be *The*

*Paradise Restaurant.* He watched them head around to the side of the building.

Where could he ditch the car? There were no open parking spaces and he didn't want to risk leaving the Camry double parked. A branch bank appeared up ahead and, with great relief, he pulled into their parking lot. Hopefully, no one would notice that he wasn't a customer. He used his book as cover when he slipped his gun out of the glove compartment and into the back waistband of his pants, covering it again with his jacket. No pedestrians seemed to notice him as he trotted back to the restaurant and headed nonchalantly up the driveway to the side entrance. An intercom with a camera was labelled Cormier/Reid, with a plaque under it directing "restaurant deliveries to back door." Lawrence eyed a small label on one of the top glass door panels which read "Top Dog Security". From the large second-floor windows he'd observed, the couple probably lived up there in an apartment. And, he bet, that that was where Ash Burke was hiding.

# Chapter 57

Back in his car, Lawrence googled the Paradise Restaurant on his phone and instantly found the Boston Magazine article about its superstar chef-owner, Luc Cormier. He pinch-and-zoomed a photo to confirm that this was the blond guy that he had followed. The article stated that Cormier and his partner, Iris Reid, lived above the restaurant. He still didn't know how those two were connected to Ash Burke, but Mother Burke's handover of art supplies to them and the girlfriend's comment strongly implied that this couple was sheltering Terry's murderer. And as it was Saturday afternoon, Cormier would probably be tied up in the restaurant kitchen busy with cooking prep.

Thanks to Top Dog Security, Lawrence would have to go old-school to get in. He'd spent the last two days driving around shopping malls in Woburn, putting together the tools he thought he might need. A glass-cutter and lock picks were already in his duffle bag, but there was no way he could get his hands on a Wi-Fi jammer to block the signal between the security control panel and the alarm sensors. He'd picked up enough knowledge in prison to know how hard those were to find on short notice.

The Brattle Square Florist was located in Harvard Square, which meant that parking would be another nightmare. How did people live in this ridiculous city? He circled the busy blocks for twenty minutes before seeing a car's brake lights up ahead, signaling a spot opening up. He used the few quarters he had in the meter. A powerful earthy floral smell hit him as he entered the store and he headed toward the pre-made holiday displays. He grabbed a tall bushy arrangement and laid it down by the cash register.

"Would you like a gift card with that?" the young woman behind the counter asked as she wrapped up his flowers, tying a thick red ribbon around the base.

"Good idea," Lawrence slipped two twenties out of his wallet, took the card and printed in large letters, *Thanks for your help today. Love, Ellie.* Yeah, the redhead looked like the type to sign her notes with "love". He taped it to the front of the cellophane wrapping.

When he drove back to the handy bank parking lot, he chose a spot in the rear, away from passers-by on the sidewalk. He opened the duffle bag and removed a pair of white overalls.

Iris was trying hard not to move, but the more she concentrated, the more she fidgeted.

"Almost done." Ash's pencil flew over the sketchpad as he studied her face, then looked down at the drawing. He made a few more sweeping movements and a brief flurry of small ones. He tilted his head. "Finished."

She got up from the living room chair, stretching her neck and shoulders, then came around behind the sofa to see. *Wow.* He had managed to capture her. Not just what she looked like, but something more. "I thought photographers were the ones who stole their subject's souls."

Ash grinned and lay the pad down on the coffee table. "I don't usually do strictly figurative stuff."

The sound of the buzzer made Iris jump. She was still thinking about Ash's portrait as she approached the intercom. The camera showed a delivery person holding a bouquet. "Who is it?"

"Brattle Square Florist."

She could see a card attached to the front. It looked like Ellie had sent her flowers. *She didn't need to do that.* "Just leave them there please."

"No problem."

Iris descended to the first floor and opened the door. A hand pushed her back hard into the vestibule.

# Chapter 58

Iris felt the blood drain from her face. The gun poked into the house first, looking absurdly long with its silencer attached. Big trouble. Karate Brown Belt or not, she couldn't outfight a gun. Her only advantage was that the intruder wouldn't be expecting her to fight back. She screamed up to Ash, "Call 911, then hide!"

Ash looked over the railing into the entryway and disappeared.

A man followed the gun inside and pointed it at her chest. She raised her hands. Iris knew it was Jones from the photo taken at his mother's funeral. Her pulse started to hammer. He had seventy pounds on her and had trained as a cop. No mask—another bad sign. He grabbed her wrists with his left hand and yanked them down in front of her.

"Jamal's father's killed your son," Iris blurted out, her system flooding with adrenaline.

"You're lying." Jones jammed the gun against her skull and let go of her hands, his first mistake, as he pushed her up the steps.

Iris climbed slowly, waiting for her chance. The air around her was electric. Her scalp tingled, and she felt herself becoming physically focused, drawing in on herself. She watched him in her peripheral vision, stealing glances at the open space above the second floor handrail. With her left hand wrapped over her right fist, she waited for what she hoped would be the sight of Ash's head reappearing.

Sure enough, when she reached the middle landing, Ash peeked into the stairwell and shouted, "Leave her alone."

Sheba let out a deep howl.

When Jones reflexively raised the gun away from Iris' head toward the noise, Iris smashed her elbow hard into the bridge of his nose, making a sound like ice cracking. He reached for his nose, dropping the gun. It clattered down the steps and Iris dove for it, but Jones kicked her in the ribs as she passed. He grabbed her, lifted her up and jammed her against the wall, his forearm pressed against her throat. She could feel his hot breath on her face and drops of blood from his nose flew onto her sweater. She couldn't suck in enough oxygen. Her vision swam. She stiffened her fingers and stabbed them straight up, aiming for his eyes. He recoiled, loosening his arm, and she wriggled out of his grasp. As he swung back with his right fist, she blocked the punch with a downward chop and drilled a *shoken* strike into his solar plexus. Momentum met mass. He sank down to a seated position, gasping.

Iris raced down the bottom few steps and snatched the gun.

She aimed it at Jones' chest while backing up toward the interior door to the restaurant. Keeping her eyes on Jones, she kicked her boot heel against the door repeatedly, hoping to attract Luc's attention or his staff's. Bang, bang, bang. She wouldn't risk Ash, in his weakened condition, coming down to try to help and Jones using him as a hostage.

She felt the door opening behind her and heard Luc's voice. "What the…oh shit!"

"Get some rope. I need to tie his hands."

"You're bleeding! Are you all right?" Luc eyed her up-and-down as he strode over to Jones, peeled off his apron and tied Jones' hands tightly behind his back with the straps.

"It's *his* blood," Iris said. Only then did she lower the gun. She had never held one before, but she'd copied James Bond's stance from the opening movie credits. "He kicked me in the ribs." Her heart was rabbiting so hard that she couldn't feel any pain.

Luc bent down and yanked the apron strings tighter around Jones' wrists. "Asshole."

Ash slowly descended several steps, holding Sheba by the collar. "The police are coming. You OK?"

*Nowhere close to it.* "I'll be fine." Iris carefully touched her ribs. "You did good."

Jones sat on a step, blood trickling out of both nostrils. His nose was bent at a strange angle. He gave Iris a dark look.

She returned it.

They heard the police sirens in the distance, growing louder.

# Chapter 59

The sirens grew deafening as two Cambridge patrol cars raced up the driveway followed closely by a wailing ambulance. Through the open apartment door, Iris watched four uniformed officers leap out of their cars and aim their guns at the three of them.

Iris and Luc raised their hands in the air while Jones twisted around to show that his were tied up.

"This is Lawrence Jones, the intruder who's wanted for attempted murder by the Medford Police," Iris tipped her head toward him. "His gun is on the floor over there."

Ash descended the rest of the staircase, his hands raised as well. "I'm the one he was trying to kill. He already shot me on Wednesday."

The police officers signaled for everyone to move outside. One patrolman emerged holding an evidence bag containing the gun. Another secured Jones with a proper set of handcuffs and shoved him into the back of the CPD squad car. Two of them remained behind to stand guard. Iris, Luc and Ash were informed that Gonzalez' detectives would arrive soon to take over the crime scene and record their statements.

Luc refused to leave Iris' side while the EMTs examined her. They gently probed the red line across her throat. When she lifted the edge of her bloody sweater, exposing a bruise that was beginning to look like raw sirloin, Luc went pale. The EMTs checked her for internal injuries or broken ribs. Iris finally convinced Luc she would be fine, that he didn't need to call Arnold to substitute-cook for him that night so he could stay upstairs to attend to her.

Detective Gonzalez soon arrived, speeding into the driveway. Iris was still sitting on the ambulance's tailgate. He headed right for her. "Take me through it."

She recounted the chaotic events of the afternoon minute-by-minute. When she laid out how she disarmed Jones using karate moves, he raised his eyebrows but made no comment. Iris herself had a hard time believing that she'd had the guts to take on an armed ex-police officer. But the proof sat in the back of a squad car waiting for Gonzalez' team to whisk him off to a Medford PD holding cell. The whole memory seemed surreal.

"We'll need to speak with you again, Ms. Reid," The detective said, "But for now, you're free to go." His parting remark was, "You're lucky to be alive."

The adrenaline that had flooded Iris' system receded like a wave, leaving her exhausted. Luc helped her upstairs.

"Why don't I put some Epsom Salts into a bath for you?" He said. "I'll bring you up some Chicken Primavera from our staff dinner."

Ash called from the kitchen. "I made you coffee, Iris."

"Thanks, guys. A hot bath and caffeine are just what I need."

An hour later, wearing sweats and drying her hair with a towel, Iris followed the sound of voices into the living room. Ellie, Raven and Ash sat around the coffee table, talking and eating from a plate of Christmas cookies left over from Ellie's party. Sheba waddled over and searched her mistress' face anxiously for any sign of distress. Iris bent over and gave the dog a reassuring scratch behind her immense ears.

"It's Lara Croft herself!" Raven called out when she saw Iris. "You badass! My Sensei says to run when your opponent is packing heat, not to take him on."

"Yeah, mine says the same thing," Iris agreed, "but it was fight-or-flight, with flight not being an option."

"You saved my life. And Jones has been arrested. I don't know how I can ..." Ash tried to maintain his composure.

Ellie came over and gave Iris a careful hug. "Ash called and told us about Jones breaking in and you fighting him off. We wanted to come over to make sure you were all right. Is that a bruise on your neck?" She looked closer. "How do you feel?"

"I've got some aches and pains, but a nice, hot bath helped."

Ellie nodded toward the kitchen. "Luc left some dinner warming in the oven for you. Whatever it is, it smells divine."

Ash rubbed his hands self-consciously on his thighs and looked at Iris. "I was thinking of hanging out with Raven for a while since I don't need to hide from Jones anymore…Unless you'd like to have someone around. Are you dizzy or anything?"

"No, I'll be fine but are you sure you're up to moving around?"

"Raven's going to drive me back to their house. I'll be fine."

"Good. I'm sure you can use a change-of-scene. I'm going to rest here on the sofa with Sheba. Take the key on the downstairs table."

Ellie waved them off. "You kids go on ahead. I want to talk with Iris for a minute."

After Raven helped Ash down the stairs and they heard the front door close, Ellie turned to her friend. "Are you sure you're OK? You must have been terrified. Jones had a gun!"

Iris sank in her seat. "Once I understood that Jones wanted to get through me to get to Ash, I knew that I had no choice but to fight. He would have killed me one way or the other. So, my brain clicked through the options. After I'd gotten him to drop the gun, I started blocking and striking as if I were in a sparring class."

"You've got nerves of steel!"

"Or blinders to how much danger I was really in."

"Don't knock it since it helped you to survive." Ellie headed for the kitchen. A few minutes later she returned with a plate of chicken in a creamy sauce with steamed baby vegetables on the side. In her other hand was a glass of white wine. "You've been through major trauma. Eat some dinner, then read or watch TV. You need to unwind."

"Join me. I'm sure that Luc made enough for two."

"I'd better not. You should get your mind off all of this and go to bed early. If I stay, we'll start analyzing everything and going through all the implications. There's time for that later." She set the meal on the coffee table and gave Iris a kiss on the top of her head. "Promise me you'll go lie down after you finish eating. I'll check in tomorrow." Then she headed out.

# Chapter 60

I ris tried to focus on the latest Elizabeth George mystery but, as she attempted to relax, her mind kept replaying the afternoon's events. Since Ellie's departure, Sterling had phoned and Luc had come up twice to check on her, but now she was alone with Sheba on the sofa and unable to redirect her thoughts. It felt like her mind was picking at a scab. Jones had been harboring a blood lust for revenge and had the detective skills to follow through on it. How had he tracked Ash to their apartment? And how did he know that flowers from her friend Ellie would get him in the door? Did he figure out that Luc would be out of the way, occupied downstairs in the restaurant kitchen? And if Jones was able to gather all this information, how had he missed the intel of Bruno's confession about being the actual killer of his son?

Jones could have shot her as soon as he'd pushed his way inside the building, but he must not have considered her to be a threat. Had he planned to torture her in front of Ash to increase the young man's punishment? With that thought, goosebumps prickled across her arms. She needed to stop obsessing about this. As Iris rose to get herself a second glass of wine, the intercom chimed. Ed's cheery face filled the small security screen, and she buzzed him in. *Thank God, a distraction.*

He arrived at the top of the stairs holding a package. "I heard from my Cambridge cop buddies what happened today. You've got some serious martial arts chops. Thought you might need some chocolate to help calm you down." He handed her a distinctive box from a local artisanal shop.

Iris smiled. "You must be a detective. That's exactly what I need. Join me in a glass of wine or a beer."

"Sure, a beer would be great." Ed looked around. "I figure Luc's downstairs cooking on a Saturday night. Is Ash here?"

"He's out with Raven celebrating his new freedom. He's still pretty weak but it's probably good for him to move around." Iris led Ed back to the kitchen, refilled her wineglass, then poured a bottle of beer into a cold stein from the freezer. After they brought their drinks to the living room, she opened the chocolates and passed the box to him.

Ed waved it away. "My doc won't let me." He leaned forward, looking at her closely. "Looks like you've got a good bruise forming on your neck. The asshole tried to choke you? You know, being in this kind of life-and-death situation can really mess you up mentally, as well as physically."

"I am pretty spooked." Iris admitted.

Ed nodded. "If you need to talk, I'm here. I've been through a couple of gun fights myself over the years."

"What I want most right now is to stop replaying the memory of the fight. Is it OK if we talk about something else?"

"Sure thing." Ed took a swig of beer.

Iris sat back and considered the large, reassuring teddy bear of a man before her. Had Luc's father Scott been as sweet a guy as Ed? Luc never talked about him. Or about his mother, for that matter. "Luc told Dottie about her secret grandchild the other day and, evidently, it didn't go well."

Ed ran his hand over his close-cropped gray hair. "I'm not surprised."

Iris bit thoughtfully into a chocolate and discovered caramel inside. "Didn't she like Angelique?"

"Dottie saw it as a power struggle. She worried that Angelique would lure Luc off to California, away from his family."

"What sixteen-year-old boy *doesn't* want to get away from his family?"

"For Dottie to learn that Angelique had gotten pregnant by Luc might have seemed like a victory for that young woman in the struggle for Luc's soul."

"But Angelique didn't lure Luc away. She up and disappeared from his life. So Dottie actually won the battle, right?" Iris took a deep sip of her wine. "How do you think Scott would have reacted to the news of an incoming baby?"

Ed wiggled his head from side to side. "Scott could be a hard-ass, a little macho. There would have been a shotgun wedding for sure. But I like to think that over our years as partners, I managed to rub off on him a little and he loosened up."

"Loosened up how?"

He pressed his lips together. "In the beginning, Ed and Dottie weren't happy about Luc dating a Black woman. But as Scott got to know Angelique, he began to admire her. She'd grown up with nothing, studied hard, stayed off drugs, and gotten herself into Berkeley. She was a good influence on Luc. Scott wouldn't have been thrilled about them becoming teenaged parents, but I think he would have ended up welcoming her and the baby into the family. He felt bad that Dottie hadn't been particularly nice to Angelique. The girl had had a tough life and didn't have a father of her own."

A recent memory snaked up through Iris' mind. "Did you know about a card that Scott gave Angelique before she left for college?"

Ed gave her a strange, cautious look. "A card?"

"Ash mentioned that he found it inside one of his mother's books. It mentioned Berkeley, and Ash hadn't known that his mother had planned to go there."

Ed's eyes misted. "Scott bought that damn card right before he died. He wanted to give it to Angelique, to make sure she knew that he wished her well. As I recall, he put a little money inside, knowing how tight expenses were for her."

"Were you with Scott when he gave it to her?"

"We stopped by her apartment on Friday, late in the

afternoon, but she was out and Scott didn't want to leave it in the entryway. It was a pretty dodgy building. Angelique's mother had already moved back to Haiti earlier that week, and Angelique was supposed to fly to California the next day. Scott got shot on Saturday morning."

"But we now know that she *did* get the card. So, at some point, on either Friday night or Saturday morning their paths crossed." Iris stared off into the distance. "Where was Scott's body found?"

"A janitor found him on Monday in the mechanical room of a public housing building over in East Cambridge. There was a used syringe on the floor nearby and they found the gun in a dumpster a few blocks away, but the prints on them weren't in the system."

"He was missing from Saturday to Monday?"

"Yeah, Dottie was out of her mind with worry. The force had everyone out looking for him. He wasn't on duty on Saturday, or I would have been with him. We figured he'd seen one of the characters we were tracking in Vice, followed the guy into the building, and got shot trying to stop a drug deal. But that never made sense. Scott was no cowboy. He wouldn't have gone in there without back-up."

"But back then, you hadn't known that at some point in the hours before he was shot, Scott met up with Angelique to give her the card. And right after that she vanished, leaving behind a college scholarship and a young man who loved her."

"Wait—you think Angelique shot Scott? No way! And she

certainly wouldn't have left him there to die." Ed's voice was hoarse. "The ME figured that Scott was killed on Saturday morning but that it took him several hours to bleed out. She would never have left him that way."

Iris saw the depth of pain and confusion in Ed's eyes. "I'm not suggesting that Angelique was the shooter. But what if something like this happened?"

She laid out her theory about how that morning might have unfolded. Then they talked about what they should do.

# Chapter 61

Iris lay in bed the next morning, nestled into Luc's sleeping body. If what she and Ed suspected was true, how much additional suffering was she about to inflict on Luc and his family? There was still a chance that the two timelines didn't intersect, but merely passed each other by. Two separate events—one a tragedy, one a mystery. Angelique had betrayed Luc, to be sure. First, by disappearing without explanation, breaking his heart. Then, by keeping his child from him. Luc didn't deserve that. She needed to find out what else Angelique was hiding.

Iris and Ed had come up with a plan. She'd already enlisted Raven's help. Now she needed to finish setting the stage.

By the time Ash dragged himself out of bed, even Luc, who relished sleeping in on Sunday mornings, had finished his breakfast and was "helping" Iris do the *New York Times* crossword puzzle in the dining room.

Ash stood blinking, pouring himself coffee from a carafe. He sat down at the place set for him at the dining table. "Sorry I slept so late." He pulled his phone out of the pocket of his paint-splattered jeans and checked the time. "Raven's coming over soon to help me make chili for lunch. I wanted to cook for you guys for a change, to thank you for everything."

Luc looked up from the puzzle. "Great. What ingredients or equipment do you need? Maybe a micro plane for the garlic?"

"What's that?" Ash mumbled through a mouthful of toast. "No, I just use a knife, a bowl and a pan. We went to the store last night, and I put some groceries in the fridge. Hope that's OK."

"Sure. Go for it." After Ash headed back to his room, Luc turned to Iris. "I'm so glad he's gotten to spend this time with us, even if the purpose was to keep him out of danger."

Iris nodded. "He seems to share your interest in cooking. Before long, you'll be teaching him how to play Ultimate frisbee."

"Hey, yeah. Maybe he'll want to watch our game this afternoon. My friends still haven't met him. What time did you say Angelique was coming by to pick him up?"

"Four. But Raven wants to take him to the Fogg after lunch to see an exhibit of Symbolist drawings."

"Oh, OK. I'll drag him out some other time to meet the squad. I'll be back before four." Luc rubbed the back of his neck. "Are you sure you don't want me to stay home with you? I feel bad that I wasn't around to protect you and Ash yesterday."

Iris touched him lightly on the cheek. "Go to the game. You were there when I needed you."

# Chapter 62

Angelique rang the bell at precisely three thirty.

Iris had a Beethoven cello sonata by Yo-Yo Ma playing on the stereo. The music was quiet enough to allow conversation but, hopefully, loud enough to mask the sound of sneakered feet on the staircase.

Angelique smiled awkwardly as she reached the top of the stairs. "I'm so grateful to you for saving my son yesterday. You were incredibly brave. I don't even want to think about losing Ash. He's all I have."

*You could have had more. You could have had Luc.* Iris tried to keep her expression neutral. "Thank you for coming by early. I was hoping we might talk before Ash and Luc come back."

"They're not here?"

"They will be. Come in. Can I get you some tea?" Iris led her into the living room.

"No, I'm fine." She looked around the loft. "Nice place."

"Thanks." Iris took the chair facing the staircase so

Angelique would sit opposite her. "We've loved having Ash here for these few days. It's meant a lot to Luc."

Angelique's lips tightened as she seemed to sense where Iris was headed. "I'm glad."

"It was difficult for Luc to learn that you'd kept him from knowing about his son for twenty years. I'm not sure you can imagine what that loss feels like."

Angelique cut in flatly. "You'd be surprised."

"I've never understood self-inflicted loss. Life throws enough pain our way. Why add to it voluntarily?"

"I told Luc I would explain to him why I left. This isn't any of your concern."

Iris and Ed had put together most of the pieces of the mystery the night before. But they were missing several critical facts. Could she surprise Angelique into supplying them? "Are you going to tell him what earth-shattering event happened twenty years ago on the Saturday you were supposed to get on a plane for California? Something so momentous that all of your dreams and his were blown up?"

Angelique's eyes widened. "What are you talking about?"

"I know that Scott Cormier gave you a card wishing you well at Berkeley."

"How did you…?"

It was time to roll the dice. "I know that, soon after, Luc's father was shot in a housing development basement and left to bleed out on the concrete floor over the next few hours. He died alone while his family searched desperately for him."

"Over the next few hours? That's not true!"

Iris raised an eyebrow. "It was in the medical examiner's report." Over Angelique's shoulder, Iris could see Luc standing at the top of the stairs, frozen, his arms at his sides. Iris' eyes lasered back to the younger woman.

Her face was slack with incomprehension and shock. "Dear god, no!"

Luc walked into the living room, his lips parted. "Angel? You were there? You saw what happened to my father?"

Angelique took a deep suck of air. Her face softened when she looked at him. "Maggie asked me…she found out in July that she was pregnant. She'd been trying to get Bruno to stop doing hard drugs now that he was going to be a father. That morning, she started bleeding." Angelique was in a trance now, shaking her head, remembering. "Thinking she was having a miscarriage, she called and begged me to go find Bruno. She told me where to look for him. It was supposed to be a last act of friendship before I left for California. Scott must have seen me on the street and followed me but I had headphones on, listening to my iPod so I couldn't hear him."

Iris could picture the tragedy unfolding. From Luc's pained face, he could too.

"The basement boiler room was in some housing complex. I took off my headphones and called out to say it was me. Bruno had been dealing as well as shooting up. He was sitting on the floor with bags of pills and powders laid out, a gun next to him. I ran over and tried to take the piece away, but he wrestled it out of my hands."

"Go on," Luc said.

"I heard footsteps behind me. Scott came through the door. He called my name and reached inside his front jacket pocket. Bruno knew Scott was a neighborhood vice cop and thought that he was drawing on him. He raised his gun and pulled the trigger. I screamed and ran over to Scott. His eyes were wide with shock. He shoved what he'd been reaching for into my hands, then collapsed." Angelique looked down at her hands. "It wasn't a gun. It was an envelope with my name on it."

Luc watched her expressionlessly. His wet eyes glistened.

"Bruno was screaming at me that we had to run, that we would go to jail. Both of our fingerprints were on the gun. I felt Scott's wrist for a pulse, but couldn't find one. He wasn't breathing. There was so much blood. He *had* to be dead. If he'd been alive, I would have called an ambulance." Angelique was sobbing into her hands. "I ran."

Luc looked incredulous. "You left him there to die? He could have been saved!"

She straightened in her seat and glared at him. "You have no idea what it's like to be Black, what Ash and I have to deal with every day. If we'd been caught, do you think Bruno or I would have made it back alive to the Police Station? He was a cop killer and I was an accessory. Plus, I had just learned that *I* was pregnant too. I tried to tell you during that last week…"

"Why didn't you?"

Her voice was barely audible. "I wasn't planning to keep the baby."

Luc's jaw tightened. "So you disappeared. You abandoned your free ride to Berkeley. You left me."

"I panicked. I ran with Maggie and Bruno to her aunt's house in Medford to hide. Over the next few days, I realized what I'd gotten caught up in. The police never learned about Bruno. They found the gun he'd thrown into a dumpster, but our prints weren't on file. All it would've taken would've been one snitch who'd known that Bruno did business in that basement. A cop killer's identity can be traded for a much lighter sentence. And I would have been dragged down too since I hadn't turned him in."

Luc said nothing.

Angelique stood and looked up at Luc. "I decided to keep our child. Ash was all I had left of you. When he was born, when he said his first words, took his first steps—I wanted to call you so many times. But I couldn't risk being sent to jail. Ash needed his mother, and I needed to stay off the Cambridge PD radar so that no one would link me with your father's death. Don't you see, Luc? I sacrificed being with you so I could raise our son."

He said quietly, "What I see is that you left my father to die alone on a basement floor."

"I was sure he was dead. He had no pulse. All I could think was that I had to get away because my fingerprints were on that gun."

Luc looked into Angelique's eyes. "So, you didn't even drop

a dime to 9-1-1. An anonymous tip."

She roughly wiped her eyes. "I couldn't afford the risk."

Luc and Angelique heard Ash walk into the room and turned together.

"Mom, what's going on?"

# Chapter 63

After Angelique and Ash left, Iris and Luc stood before one of the tall living room windows watching as the sunset streaked the Western sky with impossible layers of color—blue on top-to-red-to-yellow-to-white. The dark silhouettes of trees and buildings looked flat against this display.

Iris could imagine the uncomfortable conversation that Angelique must be having with Ash on their car ride home. Hopefully, over the coming months, the renovation of the art studio would give him something positive to offset all the difficult things he'd just been through. The project would also bring him a different kind of publicity, and his proximity to Terry's death might even increase his artist's mystique. She'd make sure that Budge did a follow-up piece on the uphill battle that the talented, young painter had had to wage to clear his name.

But it was not Ash's state of mind that worried Iris the most now. She laced her fingers through Luc's. "I'm sorry. Maybe I should have left it alone. I didn't mean to cause you more pain."

There was a long silence. "You figured out what happened to my father and got Angelique to admit to her part in it." Luc pulled her against him. "Thank you."

"Ed came over last night and we fitted together enough pieces of the puzzle, but there were still some gaps. We didn't know what you'd want to do if this turned out to be the outcome. There's no statute of limitations on murder."

"Bruno is dead." Luc let out a bitter laugh. "I guess that was what Angelique was waiting for, before she'd tell me why she left. She was protecting *him*."

"Will you tell Dottie?"

"Hell, no. That would serve no good purpose. She's going to be pissy enough about accepting Ash as her grandchild."

"Angelique was an accessory."

"I know. The choices Angelique made…" Luc blew out a breath. "But I'm not going to send Ash's mother to jail."

She looked up at him. Luc just called her Angelique instead of Angel. Iris had been telling herself that this woman was the love of Luc's life. That he might even leave Iris for her. Now she understood that Luc would never think of Angelique in that way again.

After a moment, he turned his head. "Do you know what the card said?"

Iris hesitated. "Ash told me he found it tucked in a poetry book. It said, 'Congratulations' on the front. Inside Scott had written, 'This is to help out while you're at Berkeley. Love, Dottie and Scott.' Ash asked me what the Berkeley part meant. He didn't know that his mother almost went there for college."

They stood in silence, imagining that morning twenty years before. She could feel both of their hearts beating.

Finally, Luc said, "I guess my father wanted Angelique to know that he was rooting for her. He was a complicated man. I was never sure what he was thinking." He kissed her lightly on the lips. "I'll bet he would have liked you."

Iris rested her head against Luc's chest and they watched the sky darken. Soon, the days would start to grow longer.

# AN INDEPENDENT AUTHOR'S REQUEST

I hope you enjoyed *Collateral Damage*. Please help support writers by leaving a review wherever you purchased this book. I would love to hear your feedback.

Thank you and I hope you're looking forward to *Death Waves*, the next book in the Iris Reid Mystery series.

For early notification about when the next books will be out, please sign up on my webpage: www.susancory.com

Thanks again!
Susan Cory

# ACKNOWLEDGMENTS

Residents of Boston and Cambridge tend to have a sketchy knowledge about the towns directly to the northeast. Referred to as the "M" towns—Malden, Medford, and Melrose—these bedroom communities are seldom explored by their nearby neighbors.

As I began researching Medford as a setting for *Collateral Damage*, I discovered all kinds of interesting historical tidbits: its brick-making factories along the Mystic River gave the town its Colonial start; it had an early thriving middle-class Black district known as "the Ville"; and it was the site of the state's biggest bank robbery, carried out by on-duty Police officers robbing safety deposit boxes belonging to an organized crime family. I've integrated these facts into my story, although I've taken some artistic license with the description of the robbery.

Neri Oxman and the MIT Media Lab actually have been working on biodegradable structures made out of shrimp cells. I don't think they've used them to support a solar roof yet, but maybe this book will give them the idea.

I'd like to thank the following people for their help. Any mistakes or inaccuracies are purely mine. I'm grateful to the

Medford Fire Chief who answered my many questions about procedure and chain-of-command. I'm grateful to my writing group: Nancy Gardner, Paula Steffen, and Joan Sawyer for keeping me on track. Finally, a large thank you goes to Dan Tenney for his patient advice and to Pam Simpson for editorial input.

To all readers who have told me they've enjoyed my stories, I love hearing from you on facebook. Your messages bring me joy.